GAY UNIVERSITY ROMANCE COLLECTION VOLUME 2

CONNOR WHITELEY

No part of this book may be reproduced in any form or by any electronic or mechanical means. Including information storage, and retrieval systems, without written permission from the author except for the use of brief quotations in a book review.

This book is NOT legal, professional, medical, financial or any type of official advice.

Any questions about the book, rights licensing, or to contact the author, please email connorwhiteley@connorwhiteley.net

Copyright © 2023 CONNOR WHITELEY

All rights reserved.

DEDICATION
Thank you to all my readers without you I couldn't do what I love.

LOVE ON THE BRAIN

University Student Lloyd Barnett had to admit one of the things he absolutely loved about doing his psychology degree at Kent University was they always had plenty of wonderful, amazing and fascinating opportunities. And Lloyd just knew that today's opportunity wouldn't be any less interesting because he was going to take part in an EEG demonstration, or as Lloyd's best friend had explained it to him, he was going to have his brain activity measured.

That really did sound absolutely amazing.

Lloyd slowly went through the large glass double doors of the psychology building (that was also used by basically every single other department at the university too) and Lloyd had been here plenty of times for his lectures, but clearly the university was in the middle of an update.

Normally Lloyd rather liked the off-white coloured walls in the large lobby area that greeted students whenever they came in, with a white staircase to the left leading up to a lecture theatre, there were three blue toilet doors a few metres in front of him and then Lloyd would normally just go right and start walking along the long, spacious white corridor.

But clearly the university hadn't liked that in the slightest.

Now the off-white walls were freshly painted (with large *Do Not Touch* signs) to a baby blue sort of colour that was very pleasant, and Lloyd actually liked it more than he thought he would, the toilet doors were blocked off and even the large wall floor-to-ceiling windows that formed a wall behind Lloyd were freshly cleaned and Lloyd could have sworn they were being replaced.

The air was filled with the subtle hints of drying paint, cleaning chemicals and there was a slight dusty tang too that Lloyd wasn't fussed by, but Lloyd didn't want to stay too long. Lloyd much preferred the smell of his best friend's flat with the constant hints of oranges, cloves and coffee that was a wonderful mixture of her coffee obsession and perfume.

At least was good to see the university putting Lloyd's tuition fees to "good" use and Lloyd was looking forward to seeing what the building looked like when it was done.

But that probably wouldn't be for days yet and Lloyd was really excited about the experiment he was taking part in.

Well, it wasn't an experiment. Lloyd was a final-year student so he no longer had to take part in experiments course credits, which he was a little sad about. He had absolutely loved taking part in the lab studies for all the different researchers as part of his degree.

Lloyd had had his eye movements tracked, done plenty of questionnaires (psychologists really seemed to love their questionnaires) and he had even taken part in a particular experiment that involved some magnetic brain stimulation and that was seriously cool.

Lloyd loved being a university student.

The sound of the glass double door opening behind Lloyd made him quickly realise that he needed to move on and get to the EEG lab.

Lloyd went through the long white corridor with the glass wall made from sparkling windows to his right, and he just listened to the great chatting, talking and footsteps of other students as they went about their day.

Lloyd focused for a few moments on a particularly cute boy with short blond hair, black jeans and trainers. And he really was cute but he was probably straight, a trap Lloyd had certainly been falling for a lot lately.

Sometimes it just would have been nice if gay and straight boys were easier to tell apart. Lloyd was still seriously embarrassed about last night when he had started flirting with a boy at the university bar last night, only for the boy to flirt back, kiss Lloyd and then the boy's girlfriend came over wanting one too.

That was just mortifying.

And as Lloyd's best friend Jaz had heard his morning, he just wasn't sure how to find hot men anymore. Back in the first year at university, it was easier because he simply went to the university's LGBT+ social club, met people that way but he hadn't really gone much second year because he had been so busy, and truth be told, Lloyd hardly had the urge to go back.

He wanted to meet someone a different way.

As Lloyd turned a corner, went through some wooden doors and up a very long wooden staircase to get to the EEG labs, Lloyd had a strangely wonderful feeling that he was about to get exactly what he wanted and a lot more too.

Something he was really, really excited about.

***

As much as Aaron Lowe loved only having one more year at university, finally getting to do his dissertation and having the research project he had really wanted, he really wasn't sure if he actually wanted to do this EEG demonstration in the first place. And to be honest, he just sort of felt forced into it.

Aaron sat on a soft blue fabric computer desk in front of a large fake-wooden desk with two brand-new computer monitors working perfectly (thank God), and he was just making sure that everything worked.

Aaron was more than glad that he had been in the EEG lab more times than he cared to remember, so at least he knew where everything was and the three EEG caps, that were basically swimmer's caps that allowed him to measure people's brain activity, were thankfully working and ready to be used as they rested on the large window sill behind Aaron.

He still wasn't exactly sure how many people the university expected him to have in his demonstration. All he knew about it was he was going to have some 15- and 16-year-olds with him, he was going to show and talk to them about EEG and what it allows them to study, and hopefully not a single thing would go wrong.

And most importantly, the university would pay Aaron £20 in vouchers for his two hours. Which wasn't that bad actually and he was happy to do it.

The only thing that could go wrong was if there wasn't enough space in the EEG lab for all the students. Which was somewhat unlikely because the lab itself was a large white boxroom with two fake-wooden tables tucked away in the far left corner because that's where all the equipment was kept and then there were a few chairs scattered about.

Leaving plenty of room thankfully for students to come to the demonstration.

And thankfully the room smelt wonderfully refreshing with hints of pine, oak and freshly cut grass from the opened windows, because Aaron was flat out paranoid that the room was too stuffy.

In fact it was only starting to dawn on Aaron now that he was just a little stressed about the entire demonstration. It totally wasn't like he had never done an EEG before (he had only done it twice before), or like he didn't enjoy public speaking (because he hated it) nor it was like Aaron would have preferred to be doing the mountain of coursework that was piling up on his desk. It was only two essays, an introduction to his dissertation and another assignment.

Not a lot.

Aaron forced himself to take a deep calming breath of the wonderfully scented air, and it was at times like this that Aaron would have loved to call, text or even video chat his boyfriend that dumped him last week for some advice. He had been good at calming Aaron down but clearly Aaron wasn't the right person for him. Aaron still wasn't entirely impressed his boyfriend had decided to break up over text and Aaron hadn't seen him since.

But as Aaron's best friend Jaz had said, guys like that definitely aren't worth the effort.

As much as Aaron wanted to agree, he couldn't get his mind off the boy that Jaz was meant to send up to him for the demonstration. Aaron had never met the boy before, seen him before and Aaron had actually forgotten his name.

Aaron really hoped the boy would turn up soon, the demonstration started in ten minutes, and if Aaron's experience of being a Student Ambassador for the university had taught him anything it was that schools loved to be earlier or very late.

There was never an in-between.

The sound of soft footsteps coming towards the lab made Aaron look up and his mouth actually dropped.

Sure Jaz had mentioned in passing that the boy was hot, cute and beautiful but she had seriously been lying about it all. He was fucking gorgeous and like he was a model in another life. Or this life.

Aaron almost panicked at being in the presence of such a hot man. Should he get up? Smile? Talk? Didn't know. Hell he didn't think he could talk.

Aaron forced himself to take another deep relaxing breath and he really focused on the hints of pine and oak and he simply focused on the gorgeous man coming into his lab.

The gorgeous man was wearing a thin white t-shirt that was almost taunting Aaron because it highlighted how fit and sexy the man was, and the man's smooth, handsome and angular face was simply too beautiful to look at. And it was the man's gorgeous dark hazelnut eyes that really captivated Aaron.

This man was so stunning and beautiful.

But what really did it for Aaron had to be the man's hair. It was longish dirty blond that was folded over itself and parted to the left, it looked so glossy, stylish and downright sexy that Aaron wasn't sure if he actually wanted to cover it up with the EEG cap and then inject the gel that EEG required. He didn't want to ruin the gorgeous man's hair.

All Aaron knew was that this was going to be a very hard two hours because somehow he needed to concentrate on giving a good demonstration and not concentrate at all on this gorgeous man he was demonstrating on.

And that was going to be flat out impossible.

***

The moment Lloyd went into the EEG lab, all he could focus on was the stunning man sitting at the fake-wooden computer desk with his mouth open, staring at Lloyd.

Lloyd had never given a man that sort of reaction to him before, normally straight men nodded and smiled at him just to be nice, and men-into-men smiled and occasionally winked at him suggesting that they liked what they saw.

But never had a man literally dropped his mouth for Lloyd.

And now Lloyd was actually looking at the man, he was hot too and very stunning and beautiful. There was just something about the stunning man's broad manly shoulders that told Lloyd he worked out a lot, his fit clearly toned body and Lloyd was impressed that the man's chest and abs were all the same beautiful thickness, unlike the so-called typical gym body with board shoulders and a thin waist.

The stunning man might have been wearing beautiful black jeans, that highlighted his wonderful legs, and a smart-looking black hoody but Lloyd could just tell his man was seriously fit, hot and very beautiful.

Even the way how the stunning man was looking at him made Lloyd feel good, really good. The man's soft, big lips looked so inviting, relaxing and very seductive. It took all Lloyd's willpower not to go over right there and then and start making out with the stunning man.

Lloyd wondered for a few moments whether he should talk, smile or do anything. He didn't want to, he just wanted this precious moment of attraction to last a little longer.

The stunning man's phone pinged and he took a black smartphone out and frowned.

Lloyd went over to him and really enjoyed the stunning man's manly scent that he could still detect after the soft earthy notes of his aftershave. He was so beautiful.

"The school group's arrived," the stunning man said. "Um, I'm… Aaron. Thanks again for doing this,"

Lloyd found it so cute that stunning Aaron seemed to forget his own name for a moment and then Lloyd realised he also had to talk. But he was too flustered. He had to force something out.

"Lloyd," he said.

Aaron just smiled at him. "What?"

"My name. I'm Lloyd," Lloyd said as he looked at the floor for a moment, as soon as he said it Lloyd felt so embarrassed.

Aaron took Lloyd's hand and shook it. All Lloyd could do was give this sexy man was a silly schoolboy smile as he loved the feeling of Aaron's smooth, slightly rough hand against his. Lloyd definitely didn't have a problem with his man touching his head later on.

"I guess we better get you ready," Aaron said, as he gestured Lloyd to sit down on the computer chair that Aaron had turned around to face away from the computer.

"Get me ready?" Lloyd asked, really not knowing what was involved in an EEG demonstration.

Aaron laughed wonderfully. "Sorry. I'm a mess since you walked through the door. Um, I meant I haven't done a demonstration before. Sit down and all that will happen is I'll talk to the students about what an EEG is, how it works and I'll inject gel into the cap I'll have you wear,"

Lloyd just nodded because as the sound of tons of footsteps coming towards the lab got louder and louder, all Lloyd could think about was about how hot, sexy and stunning Aaron was.

And he was clearly into him as well. Lloyd was really looking forward to this demonstration.

A lot more than he ever wanted to admit.

***

Aaron flat out couldn't believe how much he was enjoying the demonstration session. There were twenty 15- and 16-year-old students in their black school uniform with their black blazers, trousers and shoes in all their different heights and sizes. They were standing against the wonderful bright white walls of the EEG lab seemingly hanging onto every word.

Aaron had loved measuring Lloyd's beautiful head so he knew what size EEG cap he needed, and getting to feel how soft and lustrous his dirty blond hair was, and he had been great fun injecting the electro-gel between Lloyd's scalp and the electrodes in the cap, and as he had explained to the students that was important so the electrodes could accurately measure the brain's electrical activity.

Aaron had even cracked a few jokes, asked a lot of great questions and now Aaron had set up Llyod on a quick computer task that could require him to learn some Chinese symbols and then say the English word for them. And Aaron was really hoping that the students could see how the brain activity changes on the computer screen next to Lloyd.

"When you're ready," Aaron said to beautiful Lloyd.

Beautiful Lloyd spaced the space button on the computer keyboard and then the students joined in without being prompted as they learnt the Chinese Symbol on the screen.

Aaron just watched Lloyd as he sat there, smiling at the students as they clearly weren't learning the symbols very quickly (probably because they didn't have the motivation to do so), but Lloyd really was beautiful.

Aaron really loved his wonderful smile, the light in his eyes and he really was just perfect. He was almost sad about the demonstration session being over.

After a few more minutes, the students were basically shouting the English word belonging to the Chinese symbols because they had learnt them just by watching, and beautiful Lloyd had given up on taking part now besides from clicking the keyboard to move on to the next one, but he was still smiling.

And a very tall middle-aged woman with black glasses, an attractive smiling face and a large clipboard walked in and leant against the doorframe. She was the woman in charge of the day for the students with all the demonstrations.

"Are you done?" she mouthed to Aaron.

Aaron nodded and looked at the students. "Before I let you go, are there any other questions?"

The students were smiling and looked to have really enjoyed themselves but they shook their heads. Thank God.

"Thank you!" all the students shouted as they left.

Aaron leant back against the white wall of the EEG lab and he felt great. The demonstration had gone brilliantly, he had gotten the wonderful chance to spend more time with sexy Lloyd and nothing had gone wrong. That was a major win in his book.

"You were great," Lloyd said.

Aaron slowly went over to him as Lloyd was still sitting in the computer chair smiling at him. Aaron felt so relaxed, great and excited about him. Lloyd was so cute.

"Thank you," Aaron said. "I mean it, for coming in today. You were amazing,"

Lloyd seemed to blush and that only made him even cuter. Aaron was about to shut down the EEG software on the computer screens when he noticed something very odd in Lloyd's brain activity.

Aaron had done plenty of reading on EEGs, brain waves and what the different brain waves looked like in response to different processes in the body. And if Aaron was reading these right, Lloyd was seriously attracted to him.

Aaron looked at him and really loved how Lloyd was smiling at him, looking adorable and looking into Aaron's eyes. And he knew that he was reading this all right.

Lloyd definitely had love on the brain.

But Aaron really didn't know what to do about it. He had only just been dumped by a boy so he wasn't sure if he wanted to jump straight into another relationship, no matter how gorgeous Lloyd was.

Instead Aaron undid the chin strap that kept the EEG cap in place and as soon as Aaron brushed Lloyd's wonderfully smooth skin his fingers felt their attraction and chemistry flow through them.

He so badly wanted Lloyd. He just wasn't sure if he could take the next step and actually ask him out.

Aaron took the cap off Lloyd and because of the gel in his wonderful hair, Lloyd looked like he had been attacked by an octopus and they both just laughed about it. It was amazing to know Lloyd had a great sense of humour too.

"Come with me," Aaron said, "I'll show you the sink you can wash your hair in whilst I wash the gel out of the cap,"

"Sure," Lloyd said with a massive delightful smile.

Aaron was seriously fighting the urge to kiss him. He just couldn't. He wasn't ready after the last breakup.

But as they walked out of the lab and down a corridor towards the washroom, Aaron just couldn't help but stare at Lloyd's gorgeous ass that was even more beautiful than his breathtaking smile.

***

A few moments later, Aaron lead Lloyd into the little boxroom that the psychology department used to as a mini-kitchen with a kettle, sink for washing EEG caps and another sink fitted with a small shower attachment so participants could wash their hair. And Aaron was really glad that another researcher had bought in a bottle of shampoo for participants to use.

Aaron was glad that the two sinks were next to each other as he picked up one of the toothbrushes next to the EEG-cap-washing sink and he started gently brushing the gel out of the electrodes with some warm water, because Lloyd was standing next to him washing his hair.

"Did you have fun today?" Aaron asked as he enjoyed the view of Lloyd from the back.

"Yea," he said, he started washing his hair with some sweet-scented shampoo. It smelt amazing.

"I'm glad," Aaron said, as he tried to focus on washing the cap instead of looking at Lloyd. Something that was next to impossible, he was just so gorgeous.

After some more great talking about their university experiences, what they doing for their dissertations and who their supervisors were, Aaron had thankfully finished washing the cap but he knew from experience that he would probably see more gel to clean off the moment he was hanging it up back in the EEG lab. It just seemed to be how the world worked, and Lloyd was done washing his hair.

And as strange as it was for participants to wash their hair completely straight after the lab, because most participants went home and had a real shower, Aaron didn't mind at all.

It had been absolutely wonderful looking and talking to Lloyd and getting to know him a little better.

"Do you have a towel?" Lloyd asked.

Aaron wanted to speak but he was completely captivated by how stunning Lloyd looked with his soaking wet dirty blond hair that was dripping over his t-shirt. He looked absolutely perfect.

"Towel?" Lloyd asked seductively.

Aaron forced himself to react and he grabbed a large pink towel from one of the cabinets that hung over the kettle area, and he passed it to Lloyd.

Lloyd quickly dried his hair. "What are you up to now?"

"Not a lot. Why?" Aaron asked, not really giving the question much thought.

Lloyd's smile grew and Aaron instantly knew what he was going to say.

"I was wondering if you were free now to get some lunch together. Or if not we can get some dinner tonight? Or if you aren't interested I can just leave?" Lloyd asked.

Aaron loved it how fluttered Lloyd got and his cheeks were bright red.

But Aaron really didn't know what to say. He was completely into Lloyd. He was gorgeous, hot and clever and Aaron so badly wanted to spend more time with him, he just wasn't sure if this was too soon.

"What? You straight or something," Lloyd said, sadness filling his voice. "Or have you got a partner and I'm just being silly. Oh damn not this again,"

Lloyd went for the door and Aaron just froze. He didn't want Lloyd to think he was rejecting him or that he was straight. He didn't know what to do.

He just had to do something.

Aaron jumped forward. Bumping into Lloyd. And accidentally pinning him against a wall.

"Oh sorry," Aaron said as he was about to move away from Lloyd and his amazing scent and he realised that Lloyd's hands were wrapped round his waist. "Oh,"

Lloyd kissed Aaron's cheek, and Aaron loved the pleasure that shot through him.

"Want me to stop?" Lloyd asked.

Aaron just looked into the gorgeous man's beautiful hazelnut eyes and shook his head. There was no chance in hell Aaron was stopping Lloyd for wanting to go on a date with him. Lloyd was far too beautiful for that.

"No, not a chance," Aaron said. "Let's go and grab some lunch,"

***

It was pitch black in the evening by the time Lloyd started to walk back to his university apartment with beautiful Aaron attached to his arm. Lloyd had absolutely loved their little lunch date where they had laughed, talked and gotten to know each other seriously well. Lloyd had told Aaron things he had never told another man, like things about his opinions, family and future ambitions that he just didn't want to tell others. And Aaron had said the same about Lloyd.

Granted Lloyd had no idea why Aaron didn't want to tell others about his ambitions to become a clinical psychologist and work in the NHS to help older adults with dementia, his ambitions to have a family and move to another country, and the rest. Lloyd had hung onto every single word that had come out of his beautiful mouth.

Because Aaron seriously was an amazing man.

Then after lunch, they had mainly sat in the same place, talked and made each other laugh even more for most of the afternoon before going into Canterbury City Centre and grabbing some dinner at a very nice restaurant. It had been wonderfully romantic, relaxing and exactly what Lloyd had always wanted.

As Lloyd and Aaron walked down the little wooden corridor with its bright white walls and blue carpet towards Lloyd's apartment with their arms wrapped round each other's waist, Lloyd realised that he had found exactly what he wanted in Aaron. He had met a stunning man, gotten a great connection with him and now Lloyd really wanted this to last beyond today and a simple EEG demonstration.

He wanted it to last for as long as it could.

And Lloyd really liked it how even though Lloyd and Aaron were walking in silence, it wasn't an uncomfortable silence and it just felt like the silence couples had when they understood they didn't always need to be talking to be intimate. They just needed each other.

After a few more moments of going down the corridor, Lloyd stopped, took out his key card and buzzed his apartment's door open and he just smiled at Aaron.

Aaron bit his lip and he started to pull away like this was where he wanted to leave Lloyd for the night, maybe forever.

Lloyd pulled on his arm slightly. "I could have sworn I still have some gel in my hair. You could wash my hair for me in the shower,"

Aaron gasped and his smile grew so much Lloyd was starting to think his face would crack.

"It is too soon?" Aaron asked.

"I don't think so," Lloyd said, pulling stunning Aaron a little close and Aaron wasn't resisting.

"And I really want to see how toned you are," Lloyd said, giving Aaron such a schoolboy smile.

Aaron kissed Lloyd gently on the forehead. "I'll show you a lot more if you ask for it,"

Lloyd just shook his head. He was so into this boy and as he pulled stunning Aaron into his apartment so they could both have a shower together, have some adult fun and sleep in each other's arms. Lloyd had a wonderful feeling that this was far from a one-night stand and this was very real.

And it was just amazing that this had only happened because he had had love on the brain since the first time he saw stunning Aaron.

GAY UNIVERSITY ROMANCE COLLECTION VOLUME 2

LOVE IN THE CONDOLENCE

Jack Willmore stood outside his best friend in the entire world's small university apartment. As he stood in the bright white corridor that shouted how modern and updated it was, he just smiled to himself as he waited for his best friend, Hannah, to finally come out.

The corridor he was standing in was perfectly warm, not too cold, not too warm and filled with the delightful hints of basil, tomatoes and cooking pasta filtering through the air from a nearby kitchen.

Jack just rested against the perfectly warm walls, and stared at the thick blue carpet that was a little silly for a university corridor in his opinion. There were so many university students walking up and down it at all hours that it would only take one of them having muddy shoes to ruin it. But if the university really wanted to buy great looking things over more practical things then he was hardly going to argue with them.

There were so many yellow wooden doors lining the corridor that Jack was really wondering how many students actually lived on this floor alone. He knew that Hannah shared her kitchen with ten other students, and that certainly got interesting at dinner time for sure, but he had no idea about the other kitchens on the same floor.

Whatever the answer that was certainly one of the reasons why Jack absolutely loved living on campus. There were just so many great people to meet, get to know and become friends with that life really was amazing.

In Jack's own apartment block that wasn't quite as nice as Hannah's, he had become great friends with a cute French boy (that he seriously wished was gay but sadly wasn't), an amazing Italian girl and they all tolerated a Portuguese boy.

Jack looked back at Hannah's yellow door and really wanted her to hurry up so the queue to sign the Queen's Book of Condolence wouldn't get too long.

He wasn't even much of a royalist beyond what was apparently normal for a British man to be. Jack admitted that the royal family did a lot of important diplomatic work for the country, they were kind and did actually loved their subjects. But Jack would never watch a royal event if it was on and he didn't even pay much attention to the Jubilee a few months ago.

It just didn't interest him.

Jack listened to the rustling coming from behind Hannah's door, and smiled at a very cute blond man as he walked past with his good-looking girlfriend as they looked with they were going to study in the library judging by the sheer amount of books they were carrying.

Jack might have been a first-year at Kent University but he supposed he should be taking the first year on his psychology course seriously, but he just wanted to enjoy university and it was only the first proper week of lectures anyway. Most of them were just boring introductory talks anyway.

Being a part of this so-called historic moment seemed a lot more interesting, and Jack would only be going into Canterbury City centre to go shopping with Hannah later anyway.

Apparently Hannah needed some more clothes for going out in the evening, and even though Jack didn't like shopping too much (he definitely wasn't that type of gay) he wanted to spend some more time with her, because with her being on a different course to him, Jack was embarrassingly concerned about not seeing his childhood best friend as much as he used to.

A few moments later, Hannah's bright yellow door opened and she walked out and Jack felt very underdressed now. Hannah looked flat out amazing with her long shoulder length brown hair that was perfectly accented by her posh(ish) black dress, leggings and high heels that really made her look important.

Jack almost felt silly in his white hoodie, blue

jeans and black trainers that were covered in mud from a wrong turn through the woods that he had taken with some other friends yesterday. That was definitely the last night Jack was going to go hiking with those friends without his phone again.

"Ready to go," Hannah said, way too excitedly for this early in the morning.

Jack didn't normally get up until about 9 o'clock in the morning but because of his own interest and Hannah's rather extreme interest in signing the book of condolence for the now-dead Queen, Jack had had to get up at the ungodly hour of seven o'clock in the morning.

There was only one person, Nick Locke, in existence that Jack knew of that would get up that early and actually function and look good, but that boy was long gone and as much as Jack had missed him for years, he was looking forward to meeting new people, enjoying the student life and hopefully finding a hot man in the process.

And as much as he didn't understand it, he couldn't help but feel like he was going to meet someone in a queue of all things.

A very special queue.

***

Nick Locke seriously had no idea why in the world he had decided to come to the university library to queue up and sign a book of condolence for a monarch that he wasn't even that interested in.

The part of the university library where the book

was located was a part that was normally off-limits for students with its high floor-to-ceiling windows, massive temperature controlled cabinets filled with ancient books and documents, and there was even an old coffee machine tucked away in one corner.

Nick was currently standing at the start of a very long line of university students that snaked around the massive library room with aromas of musty old books, flowery and earthy perfumes filling the air. There were three female students in front of him wearing red, white and blue (the colours of the union jack) and they were talking about what the new King was going to be like and what it meant for the monarchy, and even what it meant for the Commonwealth that still had the British Monarch as their head of state.

Nick wasn't really too interested in all that but it was great to see that some people were really excited, and thankfully the line was moving very quickly.

There might have been another hundred or so students in front of Nick, but he didn't mind. It was an early Thursday morning and he didn't have any lectures or anything, and it wasn't even like he had much of a routine at the moment because this was the first proper week at university.

There was meant to be something about the different social clubs you could join later on, but Nick wasn't too sure what he wanted.

Well, that wasn't exactly true as Nick seriously wanted to know about the gay scene at university and in Canterbury. It wasn't that he was looking for clubbing, sex or anything like that, it was just more than he wanted to be around other gay people.

Nick had always loved being gay despite being closeted until a few years ago, and even though his parents and entire family had been amazingly supportive. They had still lived in a small village, so he was technically the only gay in the village and that was hard.

The wonderful smell of chai latte, sweet iced coffees and delicious buttery Danish pastries filled the air as more and more students joined the line and that really made Nick happy. Especially when the taste of rich, fruity Chelsea buns formed on his tongue. Nick absolutely loved their fruity, sweet buttery flavour.

He was definitely going to have go to a bakery later on and get one.

As the line moved a lot more and the three women dressed in red, white and blue got more excited, Nick thought he heard a very familiar voice.

It was a husky, sexy voice that sounded so manly and attractive, Nick never knew that he was attracted to voices before, but it sounded so familiar.

Nick turned around and his body just froze as he saw a ghost from his past.

As Nick stared at a very sexy man with cute curly brown hair, skinny jeans that highlighted how fit he was and a bright white hoodie that looked to be covering washboard abs, Nick was shocked that he was looking at a fully grownup Jack Willmore.

Jack looked so amazing with his face being all lines and angles now and wow, he really did look so wonderful.

Nick just couldn't believe that he was looking at the boy that he had fallen in love with so many years ago, tried to date in secret and ultimately shattered his little heart all because how do you tell someone you love them if you couldn't even hold their hand in public.

Nick was drawn to talk to Jack a lot more than he ever wanted to admit.

***

The delightful smells of bitter coffee, chai lattes and the sweetest chocolate Jack had ever smelt filled the air as he joined the massively long snaking queue in the university library for people to sign the book of Condolence for the late Queen. Jack was just surprised more than anything at the sheer amount of students queueing up.

There were so many different types of students in all their different heights, sizes and countries of origin. Jack had suspected it might only be British, Canadian and a handful of other countries, but he was impressed.

He was even surprised that a group of three young female students were standing tens of people in front of him wearing the red, white and blue of the Union Jack, a symbol that Jack had mixed feelings about these days given how abusive England was towards Scotland and the other nations making up the

UK.

"This hot chocolate is amazing," Hannah said.

Jack just smiled because she had been acting like a kid in a candy store ever since they had left her apartment building. Jack really liked how into the royals Hannah was and she had been telling him all sorts of things about the royal family on the way over here.

But Jack had a feeling that sooner or later he was going to have to run away from Hannah, because as much as he loved her, he didn't really want to listen to royal tales all day.

"Jackie," a man said a few metres in front of him.

Jack's stomach tightened instantly as his stomach recognised the voice way before his brain. He flat out couldn't believe that the love of his life, his childhood sweetheart and the only man that ever made him feel special was here.

Jack instantly looked in the direction of the voice and a lump formed in his throat and he grabbed onto Hannah for support as he stared at the beautiful sexy Nick.

Even now after all these years, Nick was still stunning and beautiful like he had been five or six years ago back in secondary school before he had broken his heart and fled to live in some rural village in the middle of nowhere.

Jack just focused on Nick's thick black hair that still looked just so tempting for Jack to run his thin fingers through as the day they had met, kissed and told each other everything about each other. That was an amazing day, and even Nick's strong jawline, manly looks and insanely seductive grin hadn't been dulled by time.

"You two know each other?" Hannah asked.

Jack could only nod as beautiful Nick walked towards him and Hannah, and Jack truly had no idea what to do.

Their breakup hadn't even been that ready, one day Nick had been his hot boyfriend when he had been 15 years old, they had been amazing, in love and as head over heels for each other as 15-year-olds closeted boys can be.

Then he was gone the next.

Jack had no idea what happened to Nick. Nick never called, texted or followed Jack on social media, and as much as Jack wanted to admit that it didn't bother him too much. Just seeing Nick again bought back so many feelings, some good, some bad.

"Yea," Nick said. "Me and Jack-"

"You left me," Jack said coldly. He wanted to say more but he wasn't sure if his voice could hold it together.

He found himself leaning more and more on Hannah for support as his knees went wobbly and he didn't know how much longer he could face this amazingly hot, sexy man.

Because as much as Jack was annoyed by what Nick had done to him and put him through, he just knew deep down that there was an explanation. Jack had come up with a few theories over the years like Nick's parents had found out about their relationship and moved him to that rural village so they couldn't see each other, Nick might have wanted to save Jack from something, but maybe (and this was the hardest to take) but Nick didn't like him anyway.

Yet as Jack looked at Nick and was instantly drawn into that seductive grin, he realised that the last theory was completely wrong, because he was looking at the amazing smile and wonderful dark eyes of a man that was honestly attracted to him.

And Jack couldn't deny that he was feeling that exact same way despite all the years they had been apart.

***

Nick was extremely grateful to Hannah, who Nick just knew was an amazing person, when she suggested that Nick and Jack go into the university library's café and grab a coffee together. He wasn't really much of a coffee drinker but if it was the difference between seeing and not seeing beautiful Jack again then he was really sure he could force down a cup or two or three.

Anything to let him spend more time with the wonderful boy he had had to abandon all those years ago.

Nick sat in a very comfortable blue fabric chair next to a tall floor-to-ceiling window that the university just seemed to love for some reason. It was rather nice because there was plenty of great light coming in despite it being a cloudy day (not exactly a shocker for southern England) and there weren't a lot of students walking outside on the immense green field.

But what Nick was really interested in was the very cute boy sitting opposite him on the largeish plastic round table as Jack wrapped his hands around his piping hot latte and he really did look as cute as he had all those years ago.

"I didn't mean or know I was going to leave you all those years ago," Nick said, trying to pick his words very carefully. "My mum and dad had said about moving for years and when they started talking about it more often, we had just started dating,"

Nick felt his smile go ear to ear as he said that, and he was pleased to see Jack smiling too.

"I was too focused on you, feeling myself for the first time and just wanting to be with you. I didn't focus on what my parents were saying even when they were packing up boxes of things," Nick said.

And Nick had to admit that there were plenty of signs he had missed about the incoming move. Like packing up of boxes, his parents getting new jobs even though they seriously loved their old ones and there were plenty of hushed conversations.

"Did your parents know about us?" Jack asked smiling.

But Nick could tell it was a worried smile, Jack was a wonderful master of those smiles when they were dating. Jack was basically out and proud when they had been together, and all Jack had really cared about was protecting closeted Nick.

Nick really respected and admired his stunning boyfriend for that.

"I found out later they did," Nick said, "but it was one of the reasons they delayed the move by two months. In the end my parents just had to move because…"

Nick smiled as Jack leant forward. "Because the house we were living in back then was killing my mum. She's always suffered from chronic illness but the dampness of where we lived in all the houses wasn't agreeing with her,"

Nick just weakly smiled when he saw Jack want to place his hand on his, it was Jack's kindness and amazingness that had attracted him to him in the first place. It was great that Jack hadn't lost that spark.

"Then I got home one day and well… my dad threw me and my mum in a car and rushed us to our new home. Mum started new treatment with better doctors the next day and… she's okay now," Nick said.

Even as he said the words and finished explaining what had happened, he actually felt like a complete failure as a son. He should have seen the signs, tried to care for her better and tried to support her more in the days and weeks after the move, because she did almost die.

Jack reached across the table and took Nick's hands and his, and Nick shivered in delight at the warmth, affection and attraction in Jack's touch. He had seriously missed that feeling.

"I know you Nick," Jack said. "You're worrying again, aren't you?"

Nick just laughed lightly. It was so annoying that Jack still remembered how he acted, thought and behaved even now.

"Nothing was your fault. If anything you should be annoyed at me for taking up so much of your time," Jack said.

Now Nick laughed for a different reason. For two students starting university, Nick couldn't believe how stupid they both were when it came to love, each other and their own feelings.

"We really did miss each other, didn't we?" Nick asked.

Then he noticed how Jack's face frowned slightly and turned paler and like Nick had said something too soon. Maybe he had. Maybe Nick had said something to scare off beautiful Jack again so soon after they had found each other again.

Nick forced himself to take a deep breath of the wonderful coffee scented air around him. He needed to think about this logically and try to place himself in Jack's shoes.

Jack hadn't seen him for years, Nick had never told Jack what had happened and on the first possible moment they had for talking after all these years, Nick had basically told him that his mother had almost died.

That would be a lot to process for anyone, hell he had been for him.

"I'm sorry that was probably too fast," Nick said. "I was just glad to see you and... you look beautiful,"

Nick loved seeing Jack smile again, but he really didn't want to say anything else to Jack that would confuse him or make him panic about Nick's family. Nick had done enough and explained why he had effectively abandoned Jack all those years ago.

His job was done.

So Nick stood up, grabbed his coffee and kissed Jack on the head. He loved the feeling of Jack's smooth skin and it really did remind him of old amazing times, then Nick started to walk away when Jack grabbed his hand so hard that some of Nick's coffee spilt on his shirt.

"What are you doing today?" Jack asked rather quick and Nick could have sworn there was an edge of desperation to his voice.

Nick just smiled. "Whatever you want me to do,"

Jack just smiled and pulled him closer for another kiss.

***

Jack was completely amazed how today had gone since he had met the love of his life again at 9 o'clock in the morning. They had spent all morning in the library café talking, laughing and catching up about themselves, and Jack couldn't believe how wonderful it was to laugh as much as Nick made him again.

He had really missed that.

Then Jack and Nick had gone down into Canterbury City Centre to have lunch, walk about the shops (without buying anything of course) and Jack was surprised to realise just how natural and right it felt to have gorgeous Nick by his side. There was never an awkward moment between them and it honestly felt like they had been boyfriends for years, maybe even forever.

Jack had loved it even more when Hannah had joined them for dinner and Jack was laughing so much because of Hannah and Nick's constant bantering that his jaw still hurt even now, and Jack and Nick had even shared a sundae dessert together and that simple thing meant the entire world to Jack.

It really had been magical.

Now at nine o'clock at night, Jack was impressed by the silence of the university library with only distant talking and tapping of computer keys for comfort as him and beautiful Nick stood in the chamber where the Book of Condolence for the late Queen was contained.

There weren't any more students here queueing up, there was no longer the great aromas of chai lattes, coffee and perfumes from other students. It was just Jack, the love of his life and the strange death that had ultimately bought them together again.

Because the weirdest thing about all of this was, Jack honestly didn't know if he would have seen Nick again if the Queen hadn't of died and the university had arranged for a book of condolence so students could write messages about the Queen once more. They both had different courses, different friends and slightly different lives.

So maybe this condolence book was actually a good thing, so Jack wrapped his thin fingers around Nick's amazingly warm and caring hand then they both went over to the book that was standing on a tall table with pens for students to write with.

Jack was impressed that it was a coffee-table sized book with plenty of endearing, supportive and almost heart-breaking messages of love for the Queen. Jack was amazed and really honoured to be British at that moment because they really did love the amazing monarch that had loved them too.

Jack picked up a cold pen and wrote a very simple message but a message that was true and very appropriate for the love story this moment had started, and hopefully it would never end again.

Thanks for bringing us together again.

Nick slowly turned Jack again and kissed him on the lips, the first time in hours, and Jack had missed the feeling of Nick's soft smooth lips against him.

And he instantly realised that no matter what happened today, tomorrow or even a month from now, their love would probably make it and that really, really excited him for the future. And it was strange how it all happened because of a monarch's death and the need to share their condolences.

A very strange but magical meet-cue for the history books for sure.

A ROMANTIC DROP AT UNIVERSITY
28th September 2022
Canterbury, England

Part-Time MI5 Intelligence Officer Jeremy Clarkes absolutely loved the massive sofa he lowered himself onto with its large red cushions that basically absorbed his small body, the very comfortable black fabric that was slightly cold to the touch that wrapped around his lower region and he really enjoy the peace and quiet of the wide long wooden hallway he was in.

The hallway itself probably wasn't anything too special to the university students that came here each and every day, and Jeremy supposed when he had been a student here at Kent University, this long and very wide corridor with its smooth wooden walls to the left, a few wooden doors that led into grand music halls and on the right there were massive floor-to-ceiling windows, he hadn't cared either.

Maybe the so-called grand designer of the university believed the floor-to-ceiling windows were meant to be nice, beautiful or impressive. But in reality it was a minor shame that the windows only looked out onto a narrow concrete path between this building and another grey university building that Jeremy believed was the biology building.

But Jeremy was hardly going to hold the sheer lack of view against the designer, because the wide, long wooden corridor was rather nice and Jeremy was more than happy to wait here until his contact came to meet him.

The air smelt wonderful with great thick aromas of bitter coffee, sweet creamy cakes and even the amazing smell of juicy crispy bacon came from the little university restaurant at the far end of the corridor past some stairs, groups of students and the half-broken wooden door to another lecture theatre.

The great sound of students talking, laughing and debating how unfair their coursework was this term just made Jeremy smile, because he had been out of university for a few years now after studying psychology (which wasn't profiling like every single person believed that really did annoy Jeremy) and he was working part-time on his Master degree whilst helping out MI5 at the same time.

Jeremy really loved how his dad had wanted him to work for MI5 and work for his department, but Jeremy had really wanted to get his Masters in clinical psychology (or mental health as Jeremy explained to everyone else) so instead Jeremy's dad *bullied* (more like pleaded) for Jeremy to work part time for MI5.

So Jeremy agreed.

Granted Jeremy never believed he would have to return to his old university to meet a contact that meant to be giving him a memory stick containing information. Since apparently MI5 believed one of the professors at the University was meant to be selling secrets to the Russians because Kent University had a number of top-secret government contracts.

Jeremy had to admit his old university was impressive as hell because they had managed to get government contracts on a range of issues, like cybersecurity, research new materials for body armour and even highly advanced communications systems.

It was great that Kent University was doing this sort of work but Jeremy was a little concerned that there was a possible enemy operative in the university.

Ideally Jeremy would have liked his dad to give him the mission of *deposing* of the threat to national security but apparently his dad didn't believe he was ready for that sort of responsibility.

Jeremy completely disagreed, because Jeremy had slept with enemy agents to get classified Brazilian, French and Spanish intelligence and he had even had to kill a few of them by *accident*, so Jeremy just couldn't understand why he wasn't allowed to end this threat to national security.

The beautiful sound of two men laughing as they walked past made Jeremy smile a little, and Jeremy had to admit they really did look beautiful in their dark blue jeans, blue jumpers and smooth round faces.

Jeremy had seriously missed the university scene for young men, and university had actually been an amazing time for him. He had first learnt he was gay here, he had lost his virginity and he had really learnt the sort of person who he wanted to be.

Granted no one here would have been able to tell he was gay or even an intelligence officer, because he had really tried for the student-look today, or at least what he called the student-look. Some tight sexy blue jeans, a white t-shirt that showed how slim he was and some black trainers.

It might not have been as attractive as the sporty men walking around university with their sportswear, but Jeremy knew he looked pretty cute, and judging by the range of looks he had gotten earlier from men and women he sort of knew that he was completely right.

Jeremy checked the time on his black smartphone and it was coming up to midday, and Jeremy just really hoped that the contact he was meeting would show up soon.

He still had a lot of reading to do for his Masters degree after this meeting and after he had travelled to see his dad to hand over the memory stick.

Jeremy just really hoped that the contact wouldn't be too long because the longer MI5 didn't have that memory stick, the longer that foul rogue professor was out on the streets selling information to the Russians.

And Jeremy just knew from personal experience how deadly that really was.

***

28th September 2022

Canterbury, England

PhD Student William Conner leant against the slightly cold red brick wall of a very large and very long glass building that housed the university's libraries with tens of thousands of books and several cafes and workstations for students where William studied. He really liked the slight coldness that radiated through his white shirt, chequered blue trousers and his brown shoes.

He just felt like he needed the coldness more than anything today, and he really wasn't sure if he was doing the right thing.

William just focused on the constantly moving sea of students in all their different heights, weights and ethnic origins flow up and down the brick path ahead of him. He didn't recognise any of them at all but that was hardly surprising considering it was the first week back at university for everyone, so there were thousands of new students that had just joined.

But at least there were some cute boys that William didn't recognise. There was one very cute boy that might have been 22 or 23, just a year or two younger than himself, with longish brown hair and a perfectly round face that was walking towards the library.

The crisp, refreshing and slightly damp air surrounded William as he felt a little excited for a moment until the cute boy smiled and kissed his girlfriend, and William just laughed a little.

All the students were talking to each other, catching up on their summers, what they wanted out of this year and what they thought of their courses so far. It was so amazing to hear so many voices again and it really was like the university campus was finally back to normal after the eerie silence of the summer months.

But William just realised he must have been kidding himself if he seriously believed that dating would actually be any easier this year. He was 24 years old, bisexual and he had barely been able to do too much dating in recent years.

He seriously loved women but after dating a few last years and in his Masters and Undergraduate degrees, he just wanted to try dating a man. He had only dated one seriously hot guy in High school but that had ended awfully.

Yet the problem was always the same for all gay or bisexual people, William just had absolutely no clue how the hell he was going to meet a hot cute man to fall in love with. It was seriously the bane of his life, and he had wondered about going to the university's LGBT+ society on Friday but that just didn't seem like his sort of thing.

He tried to just forget about his dating problems as he looked at the time on his large blue smartphone and it was starting to approach midday. He still couldn't believe that he was actually meant to be meeting a spy or Intelligence Officer as they preferred to be called to hand over a memory stick.

William still felt so guilty about it all, and he really didn't want to do it, because Professor Davenport had seriously been so great to William, without Davenport William really doubted he would have gotten onto the PhD position (because of department politics for than anything else) and the professor had been a great supervisor.

It just seemed so wrong of William to hand over the memory stick and all the information that could get the professor arrested or even worse, killed.

But William had to hand over the stupid memory stick more than anything else in the world, his father had been murdered by Russia-backed insurrectionists in Afghanistan so William was not allowing the damn pathetic Russians to hurt him anymore.

And if the price to protect the UK, like his father would have wanted, was to make a "good" man go to prison then that was okay to William. It just had to be okay.

William took a deep breath of the crisp, refreshing air and took a few steps forward and merged with the endless stream of the students going in and out of the library and past it.

William just kept following the brick path ahead of him, trying not to knock into the other students as he hooked a left onto another brick path towards the university building he was meant to be meeting the Intelligence Officer in.

He didn't even know what the officer looked like, he didn't know if he was expecting James Bond, a man in a suit or street clothes or anything. William was completely in the dark, and part of him just wanted the man or woman to be hot.

That wouldn't be a problem.

But William forced himself not to get his hopes up as most intelligence officers were probably older men and women in their 30s or older. A little out of William's age range but he seriously wished the officer would be hot.

And just because he had read a few spy novels last night (something he fully admitted he should not have done because the informant always dies in them) and learnt that a lot of contacts get pickpocketed before dying, William placed his hands in his jean pockets.

Thankfully the small black memory stick was still in there so William simply wrapped his fingers around it.

After a few more moments of walking along the long brick path and got to a very modern-looking wooden university building, William went through some glass doors, hooked a right and went down a very wide and long corridor with massive sofas and smooth wooden walls to his left and horrible floor-to-ceiling windows to his right.

William really didn't like the windows because

they were so awful, tasteless and the designer had to be an idiot because of the sheer lack of view and-

William stopped dead in his tracks as he looked at the most beautiful man he had ever seen sitting on one of the large black sofas in the corridor.

The man was so hot and beautiful and sexy with his white t-shirt that showed how seriously fit he was, his tight blue jeans that only amplified his raw sexual appeal even more and William really, really loved the man's cute little square face that looked so young and innocent but there was just something about his eyes.

Maybe other students here looked at the hot sexy man and presumed he was another student that was innocent in the ways of the world, but William just recognised something.

A certain type of emotional damage or experience behind the hot man's sexy emerald eyes that made William instantly know that the beautiful man was the intelligence officer he was meant to be meeting.

And William couldn't help but realise the hot man was a little young, maybe only a year younger than him, William had absolutely no problem with hopefully getting to know this sexy, hot, beautiful man a little better.

And that all came with the hopeful bonus of helping to protect the UK as well.

***

28th September 2022
Canterbury, England

As much as Jeremy loved the amazing softness of the large black sofa with its pillows and wonderful fabric, Jeremy was seriously starting to wonder if this contact would ever show up, and even worse what if the entire mission had been compromised?

That had already happened to Jeremy far more times than he actually wanted to think about. The last time in Paris with the French DGSE, the Italian Mob and a scared cute man was not Jeremy's idea of fun in the slightest, so Jeremy just really hoped that the mission was fine.

As it was lunchtime, the sound of students talking, moving and catching up on their summers got louder and louder as more students came into the university building and dived into the restaurant at the far end of the corridor, but they were all so loud that the sound carried perfectly.

Jeremy was about to move further up the wooden corridor to another large black sofa when he noticed someone coming towards him. He couldn't see who it was exactly because they were sort of merged into the endless stream of students coming into the corridor.

If this person had intelligence training then Jeremy had to admit they were excellent, because they would be far too close to Jeremy for comfort before he had properly assessed if they were a threat or not.

But then he actually saw the guy.

The second the hot sexy guy stepped into perfect view Jeremy was just shocked to the core.

He had absolutely no idea how the hot sexy guy could look so average and rather unappealing in the few photos and pieces of paper that his father had given him, but in reality the guy actually looked like a god.

Jeremy seriously loved the guy's amazing looking legs in his jeans, the crisp white shirt that made him look so intelligent, clever and sexy with the wonderful added bonus of it showing how slim the guy was underneath.

And Jeremy seriously loved how cute the guy was with his longish fluffy brown hair that he really, really wanted to run his fingers through, his slight brown beard and Jeremy just knew the guy's smooth, youthful face was simply adorable.

The guy was sheer perfection and probably one of the most beautiful guys Jeremy had actually ever seen, and that included a lot of foreign agents trying to attack the UK.

Jeremy felt his hands turn sweaty and he felt sweat slowly roll down his back and his wayward parts flare to life as he stared at the sexy hunk of a guy that was walking towards him.

Then the hot sexy guy simply came over to him and held out the little black memory stick that contained all the information to save or damn the UK.

The hot sexy guy didn't ask if Jeremy was the Officer he was meant to meet, he didn't know if Jeremy was friendly and Jeremy was just shocked at him.

If he had been anyone else in the slightest, Jeremy would have been mad, a little annoyed and so infuriated that a person with no intelligence training could have destroyed UK national security by making such a simple mistake.

Jeremy just couldn't believe this hot sexy guy had been willing to hand over the memory stick so easily. What if Jeremy had been working for the professor or the Russians?

But as much as Jeremy wanted to be annoyed with this very cute fool, he actually couldn't bring himself to be any of that. All he could do was simply stare into the beautifully soft brown eyes of this guy and really want to know more about him.

Yet he had a job to do first.

Jeremy gently smiled and shook his head as he took the memory stick of the guy, making sure their fingers grazed each other for a moment. And Jeremy seriously loved the smoothness and tenderness of the guy's warm, slightly sweaty, skin against his own.

And Jeremy could have sworn he felt the beautiful guy's fingers stretch out a little more as if they both never wanted this moment to end and they both wanted to hold each other's hands for a little longer.

Jeremy really wanted that, more than anything else in the entire world at the moment actually, but he sadly forced himself to pull away and took out his black smartphone.

One of the same benefits of working for MI5 was that Jeremy got access to a lot of great apps that he really loved, including a smartphone app that allowed him to scan memory sticks without them having to be plugged in. He had absolutely no idea how it worked but it was an amazing app for sure.

"What's that?" the guy asked.

Jeremy smiled at him and he felt his smile turn into a sexy grin as he looked at the amazing guy in front of him.

When he had met informants or contacts before, they were normally so scared, concerned or nervous, but this guy wasn't. That could have meant that the guy had no idea what he was actually involved in, but as he was doing a PhD Jeremy really doubted he was that stupid.

Or this amazing guy was clearly curious and Jeremy really liked that in a guy.

Jeremy gestured for both of them to sit down on the large black sofa and the guy slowly nodded and they both did.

Jeremy was fairly sure that if he looked at any MI5 policy or rulebook, he wasn't meant to sit back down once he had the asset (the memory stick) in case they were attacked and technically his mission now was to validate the memory stick was real and get it as soon as possible to MI5.

But around this really hot sexy guy, Jeremy just didn't want to leave yet and he even wanted to get to know this beautiful guy a little more.

"Can I know you're name?" the hot sexy guy asked.

Jeremy smiled. He said it so nervously and with such a schoolboy grin that the guy looked so cute and Jeremy was slightly willing to bend a rule or two for this cutie.

"Only my first name but I'm Jeremy," he said holding out his hand.

The guy unleashed another sexy schoolboy grin that melted Jeremy's heart but Jeremy hated it when he had to take back his hand before the guy shook it because his phone buzzed.

"I'm William," the hot guy said.

"Hot name," Jeremy said, regretting it the moment he said it. "Um, sorry I'm normally more professional than this,"

Jeremy really couldn't believe he had actually just said that to a contact, he hated being so unprofessional but this guy was just so cute.

Then it hit Jeremy that he really needed to make himself not like this guy. MI5 Officers couldn't fall for contacts or anything, it was the rules and this guy was a PhD student and he was only a Masters student.

They weren't exactly compatible.

Jeremy forced his attention back to his phone and smiled that the memory stick did actually contain all the information MI5 needed.

"Wow," Jeremy said as he scrolled through some of the data. "This is amazing. This contains email addresses, bank accounts and details every little document the professor sent,"

Jeremy just looked at sexy William and smiled. He had met some good and great contacts before during his part-time intelligence work but William might be the best. He had never seen information this detailed before, it was perfect.

Just like William so far.

"Thank you," Jeremy said. "This is amazing,"

William shrugged like it was nothing but Jeremy saw in his eyes that he was conflicted.

And as much as Jeremy just needed to leave and get the memory stick to MI5 he made himself stay a little longer.

"Can I ask your age?" William asked.

Jeremy's raised his eyebrows a little, it was nothing that he hadn't heard before.

"Sorry, sorry," William said. "I'm not normally like a teenager. I'm normally quite intelligent and know exactly what to say it's just I haven't met someone like you before,"

If anyone else had said that Jeremy might have taken it as William not meeting an intelligence officer before but he seriously hoped it was that William found him attractive.

Because Jeremy really wasn't sure what he would do if William didn't like him, because Jeremy was just wanting to get to know this amazingly hot guy more and more with each passing second.

"I do this part-time," Jeremy said wanting to be as truthful as he could with hot sexy William but being careful at the same time. "I'm a psychology Masters student by day,"

It was great to see William's eyes light up.

"Then we can all talk," someone said.

Jeremy looked up away from the black sofa for a moment and just frowned as he saw three men standing there.

Jeremy would have known the middle-aged man standing in the middle from anywhere. He had stared the professor Davenport's face too many times from surveillance footage and personnel records for Jeremy not to know what he looked like.

But Davenport seriously didn't know how to dress well. The professor was wearing a very worn and ancient grey trench coat from the 1950s, his bald head looked awful and his rough skin really didn't help the look.

Yet Jeremy was a little more concerned about the two slightly younger men with their classic Russian looks, short blond hair and strong jawlines. They were rather attractive in a way but judging how they were holding their black overcoats Jeremy sort of knew they were holding guns under them.

Not what Jeremy wanted.

If MI5 found out about this little problem then Jeremy just knew they would moan at him because he should have left already and now because of his feelings for a very hot guy he risked losing the memory stick.

But Jeremy couldn't help as his stomach twisted

into a painful knot as he realised that he didn't only risk losing the memory stick but he also risked losing William.

It was so stupid to be worrying about losing a hot guy he had only just met but Jeremy really felt drawn to him and he was quickly realising he was rather desperate for a first date or something with this hottie.

As professor Davenport took a step closer Jeremy just knew without a shadow of a doubt he had a lot to do. He had to save the UK from the Russians, protect the memory stick and most importantly save the really attractive man sitting right next to him.

Jeremy just had to do all of those things or die trying.

***

28th September 2022
Canterbury, England

William just flat couldn't believe this was happening. Sure he had been nervous and concerned that Professor Davenport and his crazy Russian friends might show up and try to stop him but for it to actually happen was something else entirely.

William felt his heart pound in his chest and he was fairly certain that something very, very bad was going to happen to them all as they all stood there staring at each other in the wide, long wooden corridor.

"Let's go to my office men," Professor Davenport said as a group of female university students walked past.

William was actually about to take a step forward like Davenport and his two Russian friends were the ones in complete control but he was rather amazed that beautiful Jeremy simply sat back down.

William had to admit Jeremy was so beautiful and cute as he sat down on the large black sofa and simply allowed the massive black cushions to swallow his body whole. Jeremy was seriously cute and William really wanted to protect him.

But given how Jeremy was the professional spy, William just sort of wanted to follow his lead.

So he sat down to next to Jeremy. He was probably sitting far too close to Jeremy for comfort but given how beautiful Jeremy was William actually wanted to be even closer to him.

Davenport laughed. "Wow. William I gave you everything, I allowed you get onto the PhD programme, I supported you and I kept supporting you. And this is how you repay me?"

William looked to the floor as Davenport's words slammed into him. The sad truth was that Davenport was actually right, he really had done so much for William whenever no one else would and he was basically betraying him.

Then Jeremy handed a perfectly warm hand over William's and William's pounding heart skipped a few beats.

"You know he's only manipulating you," Davenport said. "It's what they do and you are such an easy mark,"

William glanced at Jeremy slightly and he really didn't want to believe that everything Jeremy had said in those few precious sentences between them was a lie.

He really wanted to believe that Jeremy cared about him, was attracted to him and seriously wanted to get to know him better. But what if it was all a lie and a simple spy trick?

What if Davenport was simply doing the same?

The two Russians said something loud in Russian and whipped out their guns and aimed them at William and Jeremy.

William was about to lean protectively over Jeremy but Jeremy beat him too.

Jeremy smelt amazing with his hints of his earthy aftershave but now really wasn't the time. William had to help Jeremy get them out of this situation.

The other students sitting on the other sofas screamed and shouted and ran.

William wanted to panic but Jeremy was almost projecting a very hot aura of calm that William just couldn't help but relax.

"Give me the memory stick," Davenport said. "Or believe me my friends will kill you both,"

William smiled. "Impossible. Your friends aren't your friends. They're your Masters and we all know the armed police would be coming right now,"

As William watched Davenport and the Russians tense, he found it so weird that Jeremy tensed as well.

The Russians raised their guns. They fired.

The massive floor-to-ceiling window behind William shattered.

"Give the stick," the Russians said.

Jeremy stood up. William did the same.

Jeremy took the memory stick out of his pocket. William felt his stomach twist. This couldn't be happening.

William hated it how Jeremy was about to hand over the memory stick.

Davenport took a few steps closer.

William leant forward.

Davenport's eyes widened.

The Russians surged forward.

Punching William in the stomach. Putting him into a headlock.

William hated the Russian's rough overcoat and his captor tightened the headlock.

He hated seeing Jeremy upset even more. William felt awful as Jeremy looked so disappointed, sad and like he had just failed.

"I was going to do the same to Davenport," Jeremy said.

William gave Jeremy a weak smile and even though he could sort of guess that Jeremy was a bit annoyed Jeremy still looked so cute.

The other Russian pressed the cold metal barrel of his gun against the bottom of William's jaw and looked at Jeremy.

"The memory stick now or I will paint the walls

with his brains," he said.

Jeremy swallowed hard and William could only begin to imagine how hard this was for him.

Jeremy was basically going to be risking his entire country just for the sake of William. He really hated himself at that, William just wished that he was better.

But he was a PhD student as Davenport had said. Maybe he could figure out a way to save them all.

Jeremy held out the little black memory stick towards Davenport.

"You know that won't help," William said.

William hated it how the Russian headlock-ing him tightened his grip.

"Why?" Davenport said.

"Because MI5 already has the information. He scanned it earlier," William said.

"Stupid idiot," the Russian holding the gun to William said.

The same Russian took the gun away from William and shot Davenport in the back of the head.

Davenport's corpse slumped to the ground.

William really didn't like this anymore. Even Jeremy looked shocked or at least surprised.

The Russian with the gun pointed it at Jeremy's head.

"Sorry about this we need to cover up all loose ends now," he said.

William couldn't have this. He couldn't have Jeremy dying. He was too beautiful and William had to go out on a date with him.

William jumped up. His neck ached.

He slammed his feet into the Russian holding him.

The Russian hissed.

His grip weakened.

William slammed his elbow into his ribs.

The Russian with the guy looked at William.

Jeremy flew forward.

Tackling the Russian with the gun to the ground.

William headbutted the Russian holding him.

The Russian released him.

William spun around.

Punching the man in the nose.

Kicking him in-between the legs.

The Russian fell to the ground.

William jumped on him.

Some ribs broke.

William was just about to knock the man down when armed police officers in black body armour and face masks stormed in.

William spun around to make sure beautiful Jeremy was okay but he was gone.

And William honestly expected himself to be mad, sad or concerned that such a beautiful man had disappeared on him but he actually wasn't. Jeremy was a beautiful, hot man that he really, really liked but he was a part-time spy and even William knew deep down that surely a relationship between a PhD student and a spy could never ever work.

But it would have been nice to try and William seriously wondered where the hell Jeremy had gone to?

***

28th September 2022
Canterbury, England

A few hours later, William had finally finished giving his statement to the armed police officers at the university and suffered through even more interrogations with people in black suits after he stupidly mentioned the involvement of MI5, Russians and a memory stick. But now it was finally over William was so looking forward to going home at last.

William went into one of Kent University's many massive square concrete car parks that had rows upon rows of little car park spaces with large thick oak trees lining the edges. It wasn't the most attractive of car parks with the ugly grey brick university buildings slightly beyond the oak trees but it was a great car park.

And as the sky turned a fiery orange as the sun started to set, William was a little disappointed that he had spent so much of the afternoon and early evening talking to police officers, men in black suit and all whilst pining over a man he barely knew.

As William slowly walked past a lot of empty car park spaces because everyone else had already gone home, and the slight warmth from the perfectly smooth concrete gently pulsed through his shoes and into his feet, William was really surprised at the sort of impression that Jeremy had left on him.

William had been so cute, beautiful and hot so William just sort of supposed that it was normal for him to like Jeremy because he had also been searching for a hot man to date for ages, but he just felt like it was more than that.

Not only because Jeremy was a part-time spy (which was always a very attractive job) but he was clever, kind and he was a psychology student himself. William liked to believe that all he really wanted was a beautiful kind man that would love him, and he could love too and with them both being psychology students that would give him a lot to talk about.

And it would hopefully be a good foundation to build a relationship on.

As William got deeper into the massive square car park, William could see his little blue Ford Fiesta and to his utter surprise there was a very cute man leaning against it. Sure the man was wearing a baseball cap and completely different clothes to earlier but William instantly recognised it as Jeremy.

Why was he here?

William quickly walked over to him.

William had to admit Jeremy did look amazing in his slightly baggier black jeans, black shirt and boots that didn't really highlight anything about him but William wouldn't have been surprised if it helped him to blend into places where he didn't want to be seen.

But William really didn't care at that moment, not only because he had thankfully seen Jeremy in something extremely attractive earlier but because his beautiful Jeremy was here for him.

And that seriously meant everything to him.

Jeremy waved and smiled at William and Jeremy's sensational smile just melted his heart again, and there was such warmth behind it too.

William realised that Davenport had been completely wrong in his own manipulation, Jeremy didn't hold his hand to manipulate William, he had held his hand because Jeremy really wanted him.

Just like why Jeremy was here now instead of doing whatever for his own degree or MI5 job.

He wanted William and William really, really wanted him.

"I didn't expect to see you again," William said, slowly going over to Jeremy and he didn't even care that he was probably getting a little too close to Jeremy.

William only stopped when he accidentally realised that he was so close to beautiful Jeremy that he could feel Jeremy's amazing wonderful body heat against him.

Jeremy only smiled. "My bosses didn't either but it turns out, and this is all only hypothetical of course, but the Ministry of Defence is offering your university a lot more contracts and China, Russian and our other enemies are… excited about this,"

William smiled, he just hoped this was going where he seriously hoped it was.

"So I have managed to persuade my bosses and

university to let me transfer here," Jeremy said.

William just grinned like a little silly schoolboy as Jeremy took another step closer to him. So close that William could feel Jeremy's wonderfully sweet-scented breath on his neck.

William so badly wanted to kiss Jeremy at that moment.

"I was wondering if you were okay with that and if you, you know, wanted to get to know each other a little bit?" Jeremy asked looking at the floor with his own very cute schoolboy smile.

William couldn't believe how cute Jeremy looked even when he looked so embarrassed and shy. William couldn't actually believe Jeremy thought he was going to reject him.

William would have loved nothing else.

But what if he wasn't the right sort of man with a spy? Even a part-time one. Would Jeremy be constantly concerned about William's safety so he would take his eye off the ball and risk his own safety.

William didn't want Jeremy to be constantly worrying about him, and William didn't want Jeremy to be constantly stressed and if the UK's enemies were really concerning the university as much as Jeremy believed then surely William shouldn't bother Jeremy with a relationship. Did he have more important things to focus on than him?

"And," Jeremy said kissing William on the cheek that made William gasp with pleasure. "My father was wondering if you would like to come into the fold.

You got us the information from Davenport, I said you were great when confronted with the Russians and I… I would really like to see you more,"

William smiled a little more and his own face started to hurt as he realised what exactly Jeremy was asking him to do. And it did actually make perfect sense, who the hell would ever suspect a PhD student as a spy or *intelligence Officer* as he was probably going to have to start calling himself.

"Please?" Jeremy asked. "Will you do it?"

If it was anything else in the entire world, William was fairly sure he would have said no because he was a bisexual man that loved his sexuality, being a psychology PhD student and he loved his quiet non-spying life. But for some reason he simply kissed Jeremy on the lips.

He loved the silky smoothness of Jeremy's warm lips against his own and he simply nodded.

He actually enjoyed stealing information from Professor Davenport a lot more than he realised and as William unlocked his car and Jeremy got in with him, he really excited for the future.

Because it didn't actually matter what happened now, because William was going to become an *Intelligence Officer* and spend a lot of amazing time with beautiful Jeremy and if things didn't work out then that was okay.

Jeremy had already given him a lot of great gifts, William finally knew that he could find hot attractive men, he could finally become a spy and continue his father's work about protecting the UK and he had finally felt the start of *love* or utterly great attraction towards Jeremy.

But William and Jeremy both got in the car, and William just looked at how cute, beautiful and wonderful Jeremy looked sitting next to him, he seriously just knew that Jeremy was the one.

And he was seriously looking forward to getting to know Jeremy a lot, lot more but for now at least William just kissed him.

Again and again.

***

16th June 2023

Canterbury, England

An entire academic year later, Jeremy and William sat on Kent University's massive bright green field that looked out over the wonderful historical city of Canterbury with its ancient high street, impressive cathedral and tall spires in the distance. Jeremy really loved it how he had just finished his last exam of the year and William was resting his sexy little face on his lap as they both sat (or laid in William's case) on the grass.

It was a perfectly warm day, the sun was high in the sky and there was even an amazingly cool breeze with hints of pine, freshness and candy floss from a stall tens of metres away on the main university campus.

Jeremy gently ran his fingers through William's wonderfully fluffy hair and he was so pleased, happy and excited for what had happened over the past academic year.

Jeremy had worked a lot of MI5 cases part-time, meeting contacts and doing other work, but this was the first year that he could actually say without lying that this was a fun job. And it was only now that he realised that all the other times he had said it was *fun*, he had been lying.

He hadn't even known how great his part-time job was until he worked with William. William was still training in intelligence work and he really did bring such flare, style and sense of fun to the seriousness of a very deadly job.

Together they had found out what "students" were actually foreign agents, they had stopped top-secret military experiments being sent to hostile powers and Jeremy's favourite task was whenever the two of them had to make out to stop them from getting caught.

Because Jeremy was seriously glad that English and foreign agents and people had a massive aversion to walking into the same room as two guys making out. And it also helped that William really was an amazing kisser too.

So as the cooling breeze picked up a little, Jeremy just stared at the stunning fluffy hunk of a man who's head was on his lap, and Jeremy just bend down and kissed him.

Really passionately.

And Jeremy was expecting William to question or

ask what that was for, but he didn't, and that really summed it up for Jeremy.

The problem with being an intelligence officer that had relationships were they were often needy, chaotic and hard to prioritise over the work, yet William wasn't like that at all. He was so easy to work with, love with and just be with that Jeremy really, really knew that they were perfect for each other.

Sure Jeremy was joining Kent University's PhD programme, the same one as William, next year so they could both become doctors, work in the university and still do their job for MI5, but they weren't scared about it.

All because their relationship was so strong, perfect and they loved each other so much that they were actually really looking forward to it both.

And as Jeremy kissed William again and again, he knew that they were perfect for each other and this wasn't some fling between two guys. This was real, special and something that was going to last for a very, very long time indeed.

And that was exactly how Jeremy wanted it and judging by how hard and passionately William was kissing him back, he seriously didn't mind either.

GAY UNIVERSITY ROMANCE COLLECTION VOLUME 2

LOVING TO SPY

Part-time Intelligence Officer Steven Page really loved working in the secret computer labs at Kent University. He really enjoyed the labs' smooth white walls filled with anti-scanning technology, perfectly soft blue carpet and all the little computer booths that shot out from the main area he was sitting in so other officers could work.

Thankfully, it was only him working the labs today so far, and in all honesty he wasn't really sure why it was called a computer lab considering the only computers in the room were in the little booths that shot out from the main area. And even then, all the computer booths were shut behind monitored wooden doors.

But Steven didn't really mind the strange detail, he just loved the location because it was quiet, peaceful and he could actually crack on with all his university assignments, readings and Intelligence work without anyone watching him.

Steven sat at a large round wooden table that leant to one side because of a dodgy leg that no one had cared to fix just yet, and Steven wasn't too bothered either. He had dealt with a lot more trouble than a simple wobbly table leg.

The wonderful aromas of fruity blackberry tea, strawberry pastries and rich creamy hot chocolate filled the air from Steven's breakfast that he had bought in with him, but at the moment he was a little too busy looking at his black high-security laptop going through the various morning emails he had been sent.

Steven seriously loved having parents that were some of the UK's best Intelligence Officers, and he loved that he got to work with them from time to time with other students at the university, but he had never known how many emails he would have to deal with.

Most of the emails were great. Like new assignments, new threats to the university (because it handled a lot of top-secret government research that China, Russia and Iran were very interested in) and there were even some well-done emails from heads of departments congratulating Steven and his friends on their work.

But some of the emails were a lot less interesting.

Officially, Steven was a political psychology student at the university so it didn't sound strange for him to talk to his friends with an in-depth knowledge about how the political worlds worked around the world, but some emails from the British secret service (MI6) made it sound like impossible terrorist threats were headed to the university.

Of course, it was just MI6 being overdramatic because they weren't meant to be operating on UK soil, but they still made Steven's stomach tighten each time he read them.

The sound of students laughing, talking and discussing their latest assignments outside made Steven just smile for a few moments, because he honestly couldn't imagine not knowing what he knew about the world, the university and the threats he faced.

He loved the work, it was amazing and he got to work with his amazing friends that were meant to be showing up later, but he was still a young man at the end of the day. And it had been so long since he had hooked up, spoken to or even smiled at a cute man.

Steven was in his final year at university and he had only had one hook-up with a sexy guy in those three years, that wasn't a good sex life by any definition, and now Steven was finding that he was having to lie more and more with his non-intelligence friends about his non-existent sex life.

It was even worst that Kent University had a thriving gay scene, but Steven had never actually gone to any gay events to meet people, and with the months ticking down until he left for good. He was definitely starting to doubt he was ever going to find some fun, action or maybe even a boyfriend whilst he was still a student.

Steven's laptop pinged and Steven smiled at the email from his amazing mum that was addressed to him, his best friend Natasha and another straight man in their friendship group. There were a lot of files attached but the email mentioned something about Iran preparing to do a massive cyberattack against the university at any moment.

Steven instantly knew exactly what the Iranians were after, it was so typical that as much as MI6, Counterterrorism and the entire UK intelligence community tried to hide the fact Kent University was conducting nuclear research for the government, the UK's bloody enemies always found out.

Steven had been stationed and studying at Kent University for years and he still refused to believe the government's logic for conducting nuclear research at a university. Apparently, the UK's enemies were less likely to target a university compared to a government-owned site.

Steven didn't believe that for a second.

But there was one line of his mother's email that really caught Steven's eye, *Find out how the attack will be launched.*

Steven was almost an expert in Iran, geopolitics and intelligence work. But he knew next to nothing about the inter-workings of cyberattacks.

Not a single clue.

And with a major cyberattack happening any time now Steven was growing more and more concerned by the second.

***

University Student Phill Lee leant against the wonderfully warm red brick wall of his best friend Tom's accommodation block at their university. The day was perfectly warm for an autumn day without it being too cold, too warm and there was even the subtle dampness that made him just know it was autumn.

Phill had always loved the amazing season of autumn. It was nowhere near as awful and cold as winter, nor was it was as boiling and unbearable as summer, or a weird combination of winter and summer like spring. Autumn was a perfect standalone season that was perfect for Phill.

Phill wrapped his hands round the piping hot takeaway cup of coffee that was steaming and he was holding onto the cup like his life depended on it. That was the weird thing about the cold, it was only his hands that tended to feel cold or icy.

The rest of him was fine.

Phill waited for Tom to come out of the large glass doors next to him, but in the meantime, Phill focused on the amazing calmness of the early morning outside the accommodation block.

The large miniature lake that had a few ducks bobbing along twenty metres away was a great natural feature in amongst the concrete university campus that led onto a massive green field covered in white frost sloping down towards the city centre a few miles away.

Phill had always loved Canterbury, it was still a city but it didn't have the crazy feel of London or Manchester or Leeds.

And this early in the morning, the area around Tom's accommodation block was almost perfectly empty with no one walking along the narrow concrete paths that zig-zagged in-between all the different accommodation blocks.

Phill watched a cute young gay couple that he only knew were gay because the two fit men (clearly first years) were holding their gloved hands together, as they smiled and walked towards Canterbury City Centre. That was going to be a bit of a hike for them but Phill was really happy for them.

That was exactly what he wanted.

As bad as it sounded (and Phill couldn't believe it), he had been at university for four years now studying advance computer science with a year's work experience doing research at the university, and he hadn't dated a single man.

He had always been gay, his family had been the ones pushing him to find love and get a boyfriend, but Phill had just found himself too busy to get a boyfriend at university. Phill had dated a little during 6th form and at secondary school but he was a kid back then, he didn't know anything about relationships.

All Phill wanted now though was to have a real love at a relationship, sex and maybe love.

It was just annoying that Tom was straight, then all of Phill's problems would be solved and that was the standing joke between him and Tom.

But Phill still couldn't understand why in the world Tom had wanted to meet up with him early. They were already going into the city later tonight with some of their other friends to go clubbing, drinking and dancing.

Yet apparently Tom just had to see Phill this morning, it was so important that Phill couldn't miss it.

"Hi," Tom said as he walked out of his accommodation block.

Phill always just smiled at his best friend for a few moments whenever he first saw him. Phill really liked how great Tom looked in his black jeans, denim jacket and black designer trainers that made him look so cool and hot.

It was just such a shame he was so straight, and actually had a girlfriend.

Tom gestured they should start walking down the narrow concrete path that led towards the main campus, and Phill followed.

"Why you wanna see me?" Phill asked.

Tom grinned. "I can't tell you, but you will not be sorry you met up with me,"

Phill wanted to say something a little pathetic like he was already glad he called because he got to see him this morning. Damn it, Phill seriously needed to get with a man a lot sooner rather than later. He hated being this desperate.

"Okay," Phill said. "But why all the secrecy? Why don't you just tell me where we're going?"

Tom shrugged as he led them through a little concrete tunnel that went through an accommodation block towards the main campus. It was a great shortcut but Phill would never go through it in the dark, he wasn't that brave.

Phill was a little surprised when they came out of the tunnel and Tom hooked a right. No one ever went that way because the main campus was straight ahead.

Phill didn't argue, he only kept following Tom as they went down another narrow little pathway with bright orange leaf-covered trees to their left and grey concrete to their right.

After a few moments Tom went into a dark brown wooden building that Phill knew was the computer labs used by the Social Science Division and Phill just couldn't understand why Tom was taking him in there.

Phill didn't know a single person that actually used that building. It was often the butt of a joke because the computer labs looked like a massive shed-like building from the outside because it was completely made of wood.

"Come on please," Tom said, grinning. "You will definitely love this,"

As much as Phill didn't want to go in and he sort of felt like he was making a big mistake, he knew that

Tom was a great friend and he wouldn't make him do anything bad.

Phill went over to the computer labs, went through the large glass door and went into a room that he could only describe as a main area of sorts with its bright white walls, horrible blue carpet and tons of wooden doors that were presuming computer pods or something lining the walls.

"Who's that Tom?" a woman asked.

Phill looked at the group of people sitting at the end of the main area with their laptops resting on a round wooden table, but there was only one thing he could focus on.

Phill had absolutely no idea who the hell was the hot sexy man was sitting at the table. But by God he was the hottest man Phill had ever seen.

The man was wearing a very smart almost-business-like dark green jumper that made him look so stylish, hot and seriously highlighted how fit he was. Phill wouldn't have been surprised in the man had V-cut abs or something.

And the man had the most adorable face ever, he had massive innocent looking eyes, a killer smile and a strong, very manly jawline that Phill was really falling for.

Phill just looked at Tom quickly and he quickly realised that next to this man, Tom really didn't look that impressive.

"Who is he Tom?" the woman asked again.

"This is the man who's going to help us," Tom

said.

And as much as a little voice in the back of his head was telling Phill to run and that he had walked into something very wrong. All he could do was focus on the sexy man with the smart dark green jumper.

He was seriously hot.

***

Steven had always known Tom was probably the smartest and most resourceful of their group of three, and Natasha had only showed up moments before Tom had turned up, but for Tom this seemed very, very strange.

For a spilt second, Steven had even thought that the new guy could be an enemy agent that had forced Tom to come here, but they had all been trained far too well for that to happen and Tom wasn't giving any of the twenty subtle signs that he was in danger.

With that possibility now thankfully dead, Steven allowed the black plastic and fabric chair he was sitting on to take his full weight, and he really focused on the new man.

It thankfully didn't take him too longer realise how amazingly hot and very cute this hottie was.

The man was seriously fit with his slim waist and the white t-shirt he was wearing definitely highlighted how fit he was, and if anything years of intelligence training definitely told Steven it was that the hottie worked out. Not a lot, but enough to keep himself fit and looking very, very nice.

Steven really loved the hottie's pointy face,

slightly brown beard and his blond crewcut that looked so smooth, attractive and alluring. It was taking every single gram of Steven's willpower not to go over to the hottie and run his fingers through that soft hair right there and then.

Then he realised the hottie was actually staring and smiling at him too.

Steven's stomach tensed. It tightened into a knot. Sweat poured off his forehead.

It had been ages since a man had liked him and focused on him. It wasn't natural and Steven had no idea what to do. Should he speak? Introduce himself? Offer the hottie a seat?

Steven stood up then realised his throat was too dry to speak and now everyone was staring at him.

"I…" was all Steven could manage.

"What do you mean this man is going to help us?" Natasha asked.

Steven forced himself to sit back down and focus on Natasha in her long brown hoodie (that was bound to be hiding a knife or two, or three), jeans and winter boots.

"Help you?" the hottie asked. "Why would you need my help?"

Steven had to admit that he needed to say something to get answers but his damn throat was still too dry.

"You have an assignment to do and we need the expertise of a computer science expert and HQ has cleared him," Tom said.

Natasha threw her arms up in the air and Steven completely agreed that Tom should not have mentioned HQ.

"They also wanted to recruit him," Tom said.

Now Tom had really crossed the point of no return and Steven gave a careful eye on Natasha in case she went for the hottie.

"What the hell is this?" the Hottie asked, clearly getting more and more concerned. "What the hell do you want to recruit me for?"

The only major problem with all of this, and Steven seriously hated this problem, was that their work at the university was extremely top-secret because not even the university itself knew that MI5 and MI6 and other agencies were running operations to keep the university's research out of enemy hands. And even if their operation was hinted at and even partially exposed then this would all end very, very badly.

All of their careers in intelligence work could be over way before they had even begun.

"Why the hell are you telling hottie this?" Steven asked, a little more forcefully than he meant to.

"Because the Iranians are here. There's an attack about to happen and we need expertise," Tom said.

Steven just looked at Natasha. "Well I guess we now have to brief the hottie,"

"You think I'm a *hottie*," he said.

Steven's mouth dropped instantly as he soon as he realised how silly he had been. Damn it, he was never this silly around a boy normally.

"Sit down," Natasha said to both Tom and the hottie.

Steven just stared at the hottie as he carefully walked over to their round wooden table and Steven was really fighting the urge to run his hand under the hottie's white t-shirt and kiss those amazing lips.

Steven wanted to laugh at himself for being so head-over-heels for this guy, but he forced himself to behave.

After a moment of hesitation the hottie sat down next to Steven, and Steven had to sit on his hands to make sure he didn't accidentally do anything.

"I know your name is Phill Lee," Natasha said, "and I know Tom wouldn't lie about HQ clearing you and wanting you to join us. We are a small unit working for the UK government on protecting the university's top-secret research against the UK's enemies,"

Steven had to admit Natasha was always great at giving the official talk about what they did and she did it with such a serious tone that Steven didn't know whether to be scared or not.

And Phill was a very hot name for a very hot man.

"Really?" Phill asked, laughing like this was all some kind of joke.

Natasha folded her arms.

"You guys don't work for the government," Phill said, laughing so hard no sound was coming out.

"It's true," Tom said.

Phill kept laughing and shook his head. Steven just smiled because he had seen this reaction plenty of times and it was always fun to watch, but not when they had a deadline and an attack to stop.

Against his better judgement, Steven took out a hand from under his butt and gently grabbed one of Phill's shoulders.

Steven was instantly amazed at how wonderful Phill's shoulders were. He definitely worked out and his shoulders felt amazingly toned.

Now Steven was just wondering what else was toned so perfectly. And Steven really enjoyed the sheer chemistry that was flowing between him and Phill.

"It's true," Steven said, amazed he could even force that out.

Then Phill stopped laughing, grinning and smiling. His face just went pale and he frowned.

"And," Steven said, "unless you help us figure out how to stop a cyberattack Iran is going to get their hands on a lot of nuclear research,"

Phill's face went even paler and Steven fully understood why.

This was bad. Very bad indeed.

***

Phill flat out couldn't believe this was actually happening. He couldn't understand in the slightest why the hell the government was spying on the university? And could these people really be trusted?

Phill didn't really know how he could possibly believe them. It just seemed so crazy that they were spies or whatever they called themselves, it was so strange because they looked so normal. Phill would have imagined them to look like older men in posh suits.

They definitely weren't wearing them as they all sat around the little round wooden table.

And the fact that they wanted him to join them or help him or just do something for them was even crazier.

"Time is ticking," the woman called Natasha said.

Phill slowly nodded his head. He didn't know what to do. This was all too much information, he had truly believed that he was going on a nice meet-up with his best friend. He didn't know he was about to enter the spy game.

Then Phill just focused on the really cute beautiful man sitting next to him. He had to admit the man had been acting strange ever since he saw him, but there was something so cute about him.

"We need to know how Iran could pull a cyberattack on the university," the cutie said. Phill was surprised, it was the most the cute man had said to him all day.

"Who are you?" Phill asked.

The cutie smiled. "Steven,"

"Boys. Men. Lovebirds," Natasha said. "Focus. Focus. Focus,"

Phill and Steven laughed and it was so great to feel their attraction to each other run through Phill. He really wanted to get to know Steven a lot better.

"Well," Phill said, deciding the best way to make Steven like him was to prove his intelligence, "Iran, if what you say is true, couldn't pull off a normal cyberattack by hacking into the computer systems from the outside. The university has security too good for that,"

Phill loved it how Steven was on the edge of his seat and hanging onto Phill's every word.

"At best Iran might be able to break the first few levels of defence into student records and stuff but they wouldn't be able to get to the research," Phill said.

Natasha nodded and looked at Tom.

"How would *you* commit the attack?" Steven asked grinning.

Phill loved Steven's sense of humour. It was a very well-kept secret that most of the time computer science students wanting to focus on security had to think just as much about how to break into computer systems as how to defend them.

"This is a university with a lot of deliveries. I would infect of the new pieces of equipment being delivered," Phill said.

"Oh," Tom said. "He's good. Can we keep him?"

Phill loved how wide Steven's grin got. He looked so cute and everyone looked at Natasha who he was starting to understand must have been their leader or something.

"Maybe," she said. "Tom look into what deliveries are scheduled to be made today. Focus on new equipment being delivered to the Georgian Building,"

Phill was impressed. He had always wondered why the Georgian building was basically off-limits to students and most staff members. He never would have guessed it was a top-secret research building.

"None," Tom said looking up from his laptop.

Steven clicked his fingers. "Actually I like Phill's idea but you're thinking about it wrong,"

Phill moved his chair over to be closer to this insanely hot man. Phill got so close to beautiful Steven that he could feel his body warmth radiating off him.

"There is a lot more equipment that goes into that building than deliveries," Steven said.

"What the researchers bring in themselves," Phill said. That was seriously clever of Steven to work out.

"But all researchers are checked weekly by MI5," Natasha said.

"Yes," Phill said, "but if what your saying is true. Then that only checks if they have turned against the government, not if they accidentally picked up something by mistake,"

"Oh God," Tom said.

"What?" Natasha asked.

"My stupid university," Steven said.

It took a few moments for Phill to realise what

Tom and beautiful Steven meant but they had all received tons of university emails about it.

Today was the only day staff members, postgraduate students and researchers were allowed to attend the Careers Fairs in the sports hall. There would be so many freebies and USB sticks being given away that it would only take one infected USB stick and one careless researcher for Iran's mission to be done.

Everyone stood up and packed their laptops away.

"How do we know what we're looking for?" Phill asked.

Everyone laughed.

"We won't until we get there," Steven said.

Everyone started heading out the door.

"Phill with me," Steven said as the others grabbed earpieces.

Phill's stomach filled with excitement at the idea of spending more time with wonderful Steven.

Even if they were about to hopefully stop a deadly cyberattack that would cost hundreds of thousands of lives if they failed.

***

Steven hated the massive sports hall that was the size of football pitches with hundreds of researchers, lecturers and other staff members tightly packed between rows upon rows of stalls.

It was a security nightmare and this was flat out not what Steven wanted at this moment.

But he was more than glad sexy Phill had joined him and Phill was so closely behind Steven that he could enjoy Phill's warmth against him.

Yet not quite as much as he wanted to because of the massive security threat looming over them as Steven glided through the crowd.

"What are we looking for?" Phill asked.

"Anything that isn't right," Steven said knowing exactly how vague that sounded to non-intelligence officers.

Steven seriously didn't like how many international governments and companies from the middle east were present today. Anyone of them could be an Iranian agent or none at all. Iran wouldn't be the first enemy of the UK to use its own people as agents.

This was a nightmare.

"No sign of anyone yet," Natasha said through Steven's earpiece.

This wasn't good. Steven felt completely lost in the sea of people that kept bumping and smashing into him.

Then he heard something.

Steven could have sworn he heard some Arabic but it was mutilated. Arabic normally sounded beautiful and rather lyrical in a strange fashion but the English accent in this Arabic murdered it.

Steven looked around but he couldn't see anything.

Phill carefully turned Steven around and looked

into his eyes. Steven really loved looking at Phill but this wasn't the time.

"What's wrong and think it through," Phill said.

Steven just nodded. He was too caught up in all of Phill's beauty but he was right, damn him. Steven needed to focus on the problem and not get overwhelmed in all the chaos this sports hall represented.

"We need to find possible Iranian agents in here. They want to give an infected USB stick to one of the nuclear researchers," Steven said.

"We need to go to the biggest physics research company here," Phill said.

Steven just nodded and glided through the crowd a lot more forcefully. He bumped into tons of men and women as he almost charged towards the government's stand here.

The UK government had a massive stand trying to show the researchers and lecturers how great and powerful it was. Steven knew it wasn't but it was always good to see the government try.

There were five middle-aged men standing behind the row of silver tables talking to researchers. Including one of the nuclear researchers from the university that Steven recognised.

The nuclear researcher with his balding head was talking to the only white man at the station and Steven just knew that he was the Iranian agent.

Steven charged through the crowd.

He watched the man give the researcher a USB

stick. They were talking in Arabic. The researcher was in on it.

"Stop!" Steven shouted.

The nuclear researcher legged it.

"We have a runner!" Steven shouted into his earpiece.

The white man whipped out a gun.

He fired.

People screamed.

Phill tackled Steven to the ground.

Steven rolled onto the ground.

Everyone ran to the exits.

He leapt up.

Charging across the sports hall.

Steven jumped into the air.

Leaping over the silver tables.

The white man fired again.

Missing Steven.

Two black men and an Asian woman tackled the gunman to the ground.

Steven landed next to the gunman.

Punching him in the face.

"You fool!" the white man shouted. "You have stopped nothing. My friends will end you and your pathetic country,"

Then the idiot started shouting and screaming in murdered Arabic and twisting the peaceful religion of Islam to their messed up ideology.

Steven just shook his head because their intel was very wrong here. This wasn't a plot sanctioned by the

Iranian government this was just a group of sad pathetic men wanting to do terror for no real reason at all except the silly ideas in their heads.

Three gunshots echoed.

Steven spun around.

A gunman fired at Steven.

Steven saw the muzzle flash.

The bullets screamed towards him.

Steven started to move.

Phill kicked Steven out the way.

Blood splashed against Steven's face.

Another shot went off.

Tom killed the gunman. Presumably the white man's only friend here.

Steven's eyes just widened as he looked at Phill. Phill was bleeding. Heavily.

"Call a fucking ambulance!" Steven shouted. His training kicking in.

Steven went straight over to Phill. Pressing down all his weight on the gunshot wounds.

Steven's hands were covered in blood but he just hoped he could stop the bleeding enough until help arrived.

And he seriously hoped it would arrive soon. Steven just couldn't lose beautiful Phill.

***

The next few hours were a complete and utter blur to Phill, the only thing he could possibly remember was the shouting of doctors in the operation theatre, them demanding more blood and the massive blinding light that shone in his face every single damn time he regained consciousness.

Phill didn't even really know where he was now. He of course knew that he was in a hospital of some sort because he was in a white plastic chair with more than enough medical equipment stuck into him, down his nose and constantly monitoring him, but he wasn't sure if he was still in Canterbury or not.

Phill managed to see the bright grey walls of the hospital room out of the corner of his eye, but Phill felt like he had been parked by the nurse or whoever had gotten him here, in front of a very beautiful view of a lustrous green field with sunflowers and wheat and blackberries gentle blowing in the wind through large floor-to-ceiling windows.

Of course Phill knew that this wasn't real and it was just an extremely effective TV screen, but it was beautiful.

And thankfully, the hospital didn't stink of horrible cleaning chemicals, death or anything else that Phill normally associated with hospitals. This one smelt very pleasant with hints of lavender, jasmine and orange that reminded him of Christmas pudding as a child with his family.

"I didn't think you were going to make it," Steven said behind him.

Phill felt his stomach churn and tighten for a moment.

He was only realising now that he was so relieved that Steven was well. When Phill had heard the gunshots and seen the man aim at Steven, Phill didn't know what came over him he just ran and had to make sure Steven wasn't hit.

It had never crossed his mind that he might be putting himself in danger or risk of injury or even risk of death. It just felt like the right thing to do and Phill honestly knew he wouldn't have changed it for anything.

He would always save Steven no matter what, which was weird in a way because Steven was a cute beautiful man that Phill had only met a few hours before.

But it was still true.

Steven walked into view and laughed at the TV screen in the windows in front of them both.

"These windows have gotten better since I was here last," Steven said folding his arms and looked at Phill.

Steven looked so cute in the same clothes as earlier, and for some reason Phill didn't know whether to be disturbed or not that Steven's hands were still covered in his blood.

Phill watched Steven get on his knees so his beautiful eyes were level with Phill's.

"Why did you save me?" Steven asked.

Phill laughed because it was such a weird question that Phill didn't see the point in. As his stomach tensed and flipped and filled with butterflies, the answer was so obvious because Steven was a beautiful man that was clever, kind and Phill could see how much he loved his job and helping people. It was those sort of people that just had to survive no matter what.

But Phill wanted to tell Steven a short answer.

"Because I like you and want you to live," Phill said, only now realising how true that was.

Steven laughed. "It isn't every day I get shot at and even have cute men trying to save me,"

"Tom's cute. Doesn't he save you?" Phill asked poking his tongue out at Steven.

"I prefer you to Tom," Steven said.

Phill smiled because it was amazing to see how much Steven's eyes were lighting up the more they talked, there was such a glimmer in his eyes that was so cute and Phill really wanted to get to know Steven a lot better.

"Just ask me out already," Phill said seductively.

Steven shrugged like this was nothing. "How do you know I'm into you. I am an intelligence officer, I could be playing you,"

Phill laughed and started coughing as his medical equipment bleeped. "I don't even know how long I have left. Do you really want a dying man to die not knowing if you like him or not?"

Steven playfully hit Phill and kissed him on the lips. Phill almost jumped out of his skin at the sheer electricity and passion that flowed between them. It was the most passionate and sensual kiss Phill had ever had.

"You aren't going to die," Steven said. "I won't

let that happen,"

And as Phill stared into Steven's perfect dark eyes, he just knew exactly what was going to happen now. They were going to keep talking, making each other laugh and almost certainly kiss a lot more for the rest of the day.

And beyond that, Phill had a very strong suspicion he had a boyfriend. A boyfriend that he would always protect, kiss and probably fall in love in a few weeks' time. Because Steven really was a perfect guy that was caring, clever and loving.

Exactly what he had always wanted in a man and now he was thankfully going to get it, and it had only taken him being shot to realise it.

***

After an amazing afternoon and evening with Phill, Steven just stood leaning against the perfectly warm wooden doorframe of Phill's hospital room as he watched Phill fall asleep. Phill looked so cute, peaceful and alive when he slept.

After the chaos and stress and worry of today and not knowing if wonderful Phill was ever going to make it, Steven just focused on Phill's fit sexy stomach rise and fall under the thin blue bedsheets that the hospital had provided him with. At least the little white plastic hospital bed was comfortable, but it would have been great if it had been bigger.

All Steven really wanted to do was spend the night with Phill just to make sure he was okay.

The quiet sound of nurses and doctors and

porters doing their rounds echoed up and down the bright grey corridors of the private hospital just south of canterbury that the UK Government had agreed to pay for, in exchange for Steven not going public with it was one of their people that was the danger today.

"Are you ever going to wash your hands?" Natasha and Tom asked as one as they kissed Steven's cheeks.

Steven looked down at his hands. All the blood had mostly gone away for the most part but they were still streaks from where he had tried (and thankfully had) saved Phill's life.

"The government and MI5 are grateful," Natasha said. "I caught the nuclear researcher with the memory stick before he could use it and it was their plan to use the careers fair as a cover so in case the stick was traced back to the researcher. He could say someone at the fair gave it to him,"

Steven nodded and forced himself to look away from beautiful Phill. "Thanks both, but Tom, why did you bring him today?"

Tom shrugged. "Because you need a boyfriend. Like seriously, when was the last time you had dick or something?"

Steven was so not going to dignify that with a response (mainly because he didn't know himself).

"Oh," Natasha said pulling out her phone. "I got an email just now and we all have a new assignment together and we have a new trainee with us who had accepted a job offer,"

Steven just grinned. He loved it that Phill had accepted the job offer he had been emailed about an hour ago.

"The three of us with Phill," Natasha said, "are heading to Sweden to go to university there as part of a joint operation with the Swedish Secret Service. Apparently, there's some neo-Nazi group trying to recruit British students,"

Steven felt his stomach buzz with excitement, all the tension in his shoulders and body relaxed and he was seriously looking forward to the future.

Because he was with his best friends in the entire world and now he was going to be with a very cute man that he could finally call his boyfriend, and after years of being an intelligence officer, Steven had very good senses about people and things and relationships.

And he just had a feeling that him and Phill weren't going to be breaking up for ages, if ever and he was perfectly fine, happy and delighted about that.

GAY UNIVERSITY ROMANCE COLLECTION VOLUME 2

AUTHOR OF ENGLISH GAY SWEET CONTEMPORARY ROMANCE SERIES

CONNOR WHITELEY

LOVE IN THE STUDENT INTERVIEW

A GAY UNIVERSITY ROMANCE SHORT STORY

LOVE IN THE STUDENT INTERVIEW

University Student Elliot Pitcher flat out loved being a student reporter for the university's newspaper. It was perfect experience for him if he ever wanted to be a real journalist, reporter or news presenter after his journalism degree, and right now he couldn't afford to fail in the interview that could define his student career.

And hopefully help him get a foothold into the real world of journalism.

Elliot sat on a wonderfully warm black chair made from wood in his best friend Holly's favourite café at the university. Elliot hadn't been here before but it was great with its bright purple walls that were a lot more tasteful and stylish than they sounded, the light hardwood floor added depth and age to the relatively new café, and Elliot wasn't going to lie but he had to admit the café knew how to hire cute boys to work behind the semi-circular counter.

Elliot also really liked the wonderful sounds of

coffee machines buzzing and hissing and other students ordering their drinks. Granted Elliot really didn't like the sound of the matcha green tea cake that someone was ordering, but each to their own.

Even the idea of having disgusting matcha in a cake made the awful taste of its bitter, sharp bite form on his tongue. Elliot was never going to have matcha ever again.

Elliot wrapped his hands around the lukewarm mug of creamy hot chocolate that Holly had ordered him, and she was sitting next to him watching something behind him. Elliot had really learnt long ago not to bother with what Holly was looking at. It could have been a bird, a cute boy or nothing for all he knew and Holly could have been simply lost in thought.

But Elliot loved her anyway.

Elliot had his laptop open to on his emails because he was waiting for the hotshot new captain of the University's football team, Luca Pack, to reply to his request for an interview. Elliot just knew he was going to get it thanks to Holly and Elliot's other friend, Jimmy, basically making the hot new captain do it. The only thing Elliot didn't know was when the captain wanted to meet.

"Has he emailed yet?" Holly asked.

Elliot weakly smiled at his best friend. She was beautiful with her long brown hair perfectly straightened, glossy and Elliot was honestly surprised she was single, but apparently no one had asked.

Elliot just knew that was rubbish because Holly was too perfect not to have a guy wanting her, hell if Elliot was straight or at least bi then Elliot would have asked her out. So what had probably happened was different men had asked Holly out but she had turned them down.

And there was nothing wrong with that.

"He said he would contact you immediately," Holly said, picking up her own large mug of hot chocolate that was the size of a small plant pot. Her entire face seemed to disappear as she drank from it.

Elliot wanted to say that the captain was probably busy, but in reality, there was a small chance that Holly was only slightly exaggerating. Elliot had noticed she had done a few times about him, so Luca might have said he would do it in a little while or something.

Elliot just wanted him to hurry though.

From what Elliot had managed to find out about Luca Pack from various social media and small news outlets was that he had grown up in southeast England and he lived very close to the university, he had been the first openly gay student to play on the university football team, much less become captain of it, and he was rather attractive.

Elliot had never met the man and Luca seemed to be allergic to photographs but Elliot had found two photos of him, one on the university website and another one on social media, and he looked cute. Very cute.

"Remind me," Holly said, in-between taking quiet gulps of hot chocolate, "why this is so important to you? You know, besides him being sexy?"

Elliot just smiled. He wished she would stop saying that and highlighting the fact that Luca was sexy, she had been almost taunting him all morning with that fact.

"It's important because Luca doesn't give interviews, allow photos to be taken nor does he allow anything to be mentioned about his sexuality," Elliot said. "This is a big deal because Luca has even turned down national newspapers and international sporting scouts,"

Holly slowly nodded but clearly still wasn't getting it.

"If I can get an interview with him and show up all these national media outlets then that could give me clout in the future," Elliot said.

Of course Elliot had no idea how it would work in the real-world but his journalism lecturers had all agreed that this would be a good interview to put on his CV, and that was what sold Elliot on pursuing the interview.

His laptop pinged.

Holly grabbed his laptop before he could even open the email.

"Wow," Holly said. "He wants to meet you in ten minutes in... here,"

Elliot snatched the laptop back and was amazed

that Holly was telling the truth. Elliot quickly replied and confirmed the interview and his stomach filled with butterflies.

He was finally going to get a chance at his big break.

***

Luca Pack couldn't believe he was actually doing this, he loved students, being helpful and he really admired ambition, but he couldn't help but feel like this was a little too far even for him. Luca normally flat out went out of his way not to give interviews to anyone, even the major sporting magazines, national newspapers and talent scouts that could easily make his career and give him a job straight out of university.

Luca hadn't even really meant to accept Elliot's invitation for an interview but Elliot's two best friends were very persuasive, demanding and really good friends, and Luca respected that a lot.

Luca went down a very long brown university corridor with little and large seminar rooms jetting out from it, tasteless brown walls covered in posters and Luca's favourite features were the bright LED lights that shone and sparkled like radiant diamonds overhead. He really enjoyed walking down these corridors when it was pitch black outside and it was almost magical in a way.

There weren't even that many other students walking about. Most of the others were probably in lectures or something, but Luca did see a few students look, smile and wink at him, both male and female students did.

Luca focused for a few moments on a particular man that didn't look at him in the slightest, so he was probably straight, and he was cute with his smooth brown hair, angular jaw and fit body. But he didn't even look like he had noticed Luca was there.

Not a lot of boys did.

And even though Luca had been out of the closet for close to three years now, he just didn't feel like he was a part of anything. He didn't seem to fit in in mainstream gay culture because he didn't care in the slightest about rainbows, feminine things or whatever rubbish other people were into, but if other gay people liked that stuff then Luca would only support them like he had done with his friends over the years.

Luca had trouble fitting in at the university's LGBT+ events because all Luca wanted to talk about was sports, his sports science degree and other university related topics, but no one at those events seemed interested, or knew the first thing about sports.

Luca just didn't feel like he fit in anywhere.

And in all honesty, that was probably why he refused to give interviews, because Luca knew full well how important and big of a deal this was that he was the first openly gay football player on a national university team, and Luca didn't want to face questions about being gay.

Because he was more than that.

That was something that seriously annoyed him about mainstream media, whenever they met a gay person who played sports, had friends and did charity work on the weekends, like Luca did, they were only interested in him being gay.

And Luca only ever wanted to give positive interviews about being gay. He didn't want to talk about how he didn't feel like he fit in anywhere that he could actually meet a hot guy, he didn't want to talk about his parents almost hating him for being gay because they believed it would destroy his footballing career, and Luca just wanted to give an inspirational interview.

The type of interview he would have loved to read as a young gay boy when he was struggling with accepting himself, wanting to play sports and worried about what his family would think.

Luca came to the end of the brown university corridor and hooked a left into the café where he was meant to be meeting the interviewer Elliot. Luca had never been to this café before, he had just picked it randomly, but it looked good with its purple walls, black walls and cute staff behind the semi-circular counter.

Luca was about to go over and order himself a cup of coffee to help him get through the interview when something caught his eye.

In the far corner of the little café were two people, a man and a woman, talking quietly with notepads, a laptop and two very large mugs of drink next to them. And in Luca's experience that only meant one thing, they were journalist students.

Luca went over to them and then he really focused on the boy and... Luca just stopped in his tracks.

His heart pounded in his heart. His stomach tightened into a knot. Sweat started to pour off him. This boy was perfect.

Sure he had seen some amazing-looking boys in the changing rooms with well-toned bodies, wonderful angular faces and just amazing looks all round, but those sporty jocks seriously didn't have anything compared to this Elliot boy.

Luca just stared wide-eyed at the utterly stunning fit boy sitting at the black table talking to his friends. Luca seriously loved how fit and skinny he was with his face a perfect artful blend of angles and lines and Luca was fairly sure if the boy put on the smallest amount of makeup that would bring out the slightly feminine features of his face.

Elliot also had the best curly black hair Luca had ever seen, and Luca had to admit the boy was stylish too. Luca really loved Elliot's black and white jumper, grey Chelsea boots and wonderfully thin skin-tight black jeans that seriously highlighted how fit Elliot was.

Elliot was sheer perfection.

This was going to be a lot of fun.

***

"Oh, he's here," Holly said.

Elliot felt so excited as he slowly turned around to look at what Luca actually looked like in person.

It took Elliot a few moments of scanning the café packed with students, lecturers and others catching up before he noticed the beautiful, sexy football player standing halfway across the café.

Elliot felt all his stress, nervousness and tension in his neck and shoulders disappear at the wonderful sight of Luca. Sure, Elliot had seen Luca before in those two pictures but they seriously didn't do him justice in the slightest. Elliot really loved Luca's broad, muscular shoulders that looked to be barely contained in the white t-shirt he was wearing that also highlighted how toned and muscular Luca was with his washboard abs.

Luca's stunning face was delightful with its bright brown eyes, strong sexy jawline and beautiful short blond hair. Luca was sheer perfection and Elliot had no idea why every single man in the university wasn't chasing after this Adonis amongst them.

Elliot waved Luca to come over to them and he instantly felt so silly for doing it in such a public place. He wanted to be professional, calm and collective for this interview (hell he needed it for his career) but he just knew that this was going to be very hard.

When Luca came over to them, all Elliot could do was stare at the beautiful man that was taking a seat next to Holly and Luca just looked at him. Elliot liked looking into stunning Luca's eyes, they were warm, calming and very stunning like the rest of him.

"Hi," Luca said barely managing to get the word out.

Elliot tried to speak himself but his throat was so dry that only a strange sound came out. Holly laughed and Elliot took a mouthful of his hot chocolate.

"Right, I'm going to leave you two to get on. I'll be back in about an hour," Holly said, waving the two men good-bye.

Elliot wasn't sure if he was happier or not that Holly wasn't there. It was great to have alone time with such a beautiful man but Elliot was so nervous.

"How do you want to do this?" Elliot asked.

Luca sat perfectly straight like he was shocked at the question. "You mean, like I get to have an input into this interview? You mean I can suggest the way this interview goes,"

At that moment it was very hard for Elliot not to widen his eyes and mockingly nod at Luca like that was the strangest question he had ever heard. Of course he got to suggest it. In journalism and interviews, the reporter and interviewee needed to work together and both get something out of this.

Then Elliot realised that Luca was used to real-world reporters hounding him and of course, in the real-world reporters didn't always follow the best practices they were taught at university.

"Yes," Elliot said, picking up his notebook and pen. "Are there any topics off-limits and what do you want to get out of this interview?"

And this was exactly where the balance needed to be struck, because Elliot really wanted to give Luca the interview he wanted, but he also needed to get good information that would help him create a great report that everyone wanted to read.

Luca smiled, and Elliot's heart skipped a few beats. "Okay, thank you. I don't want the interview to focus on my sexuality or my so-called groundbreaking appointment as captain, and I don't really want a photograph attached,"

Elliot slowly nodded. It was a good thing Luca was so hot and captivating because Elliot wasn't sure how he was going to truly respect Luca's wishes for two reasons. As a reporter, Elliot knew that everyone in the university, local area and hell, nationally wanted to know more about the openly gay football player so if he wrote about that then he was guaranteed to have a sensational interview. Everyone was dying to read the information.

Also as a gay man himself, Elliot wanted to know about Luca. Elliot had grown up in a supportive town with wonderful family members, friends and other people at school, but it was still drilled into him that he couldn't possibly do manly things for a job.

It had been hard enough to get his family to support him doing journalism because it was mainly a male-dominated industry and Elliot's family wasn't sure he belonged there.

So Elliot just wanted to know that things could be different.

"Can I ask why you don't want to do those two things? You're a great-looking guy so I imagined you would like having your photo taken," Elliot said.

And Elliot almost turned around to the windows in the café in case he could see his professionalism flying away in the distance.

Luca thankfully seemed to laugh and groan at the same time.

"I would just prefer not to talk about it. I am more than a gay person, and I am not some model to lord my physical appearance over others and my parents would-"

Elliot just looked at the beautiful man in front of him, and that's when he slowly started to realise that Luca wasn't sure himself about anything. As a reporter, it was his job to make sure the interviewee felt comfortable, relaxed and wanted to do this interview completely. But as a gay man, Elliot also knew Luca was conflicted because of the expectations of others.

Elliot had been there too many times over the years.

"What would you like to talk about then?" Elliot asked, hoping to relax Luca a little more first before he circled back to the sexuality question.

Luca shrugged and he gently smiled at Elliot. "I know you're trying to be kind and you're the first journalist that's even tried to respect me but I don't know what I want to talk about,"

Elliot could feel that Luca wanted to leave but he

had to save this interview, not only for his future career but because he wanted to spend a little longer with this beautiful man.

Elliot put his pen and notebook down on the table. "Just tell me something please gay-to-gay, why don't you want people to know more about you being gay. It's fine. It's inspirational. When I was growing up I would have loved to know I could do manly things in the real world,"

Luca's eyes widened a little, he smiled and leant a little closer. He actually leant over close to Elliot that he could smell his wonderful aftershave, cedarwood and another earthy note he couldn't identify.

"I'm just more than my sexuality and that is what I want to talk about and my parents wouldn't-"

Elliot smiled. "What is it about your parents and family? Do they not support you? Admire you? Or realise how amazing your achievements are?"

Luca leant backwards and shook his head. "This was a mistake. I'm sorry for wasting your time. You deserve better,"

Elliot watched Luca get up quickly and rush past him.

Elliot grabbed Luca's wonderfully smooth wrist and he was surprised at how warm, soft and right it felt to touch Luca. And Elliot was surprised Luca didn't seem to flinch, he also seemed to be enjoying it.

"You haven't wasted my time. I got to meet you and no one deserves better than you. Everyone is perfect in their own way," Elliot said.

Luca looked like he wanted to say something as he leant closer to Elliot but then he shook his head, shook his wrist free and literally ran away.

Something Elliot was concerned he had been doing his entire life.

***

"Where's Luca?" Holly asked.

Elliot flat out couldn't believe what had just happened because he was only now realising that he had been staring at his laptop for the past ten minutes trying to understand everything had that happened.

Elliot went to reach for his large mug of hot chocolate but it was empty, and Elliot also realised that Holly was back a lot earlier than she had said she would be, and Holly never ever did that sort of thing.

There weren't quite as many students, lecturers and other people in the café now which Elliot was rather glad about because he felt so deflated, concerned and worried that he actually just wanted to be alone. But he also needed Holly, more as a soundboard than anything else.

So Elliot told Holly what happened and she clicked her fingers to get the attention of one of the hot men behind the counter, ordered herself the largest vegan chai latte they had and she sat down opposite Elliot.

She was looking at him so intensely that Elliot felt like she was burrowing into his soul.

"What you thinking then?" Holly asked.

Elliot hated and loved it when she turned everything back on him. "I think his parents, family and hell, probably everyone in his life was homophobic to him. He probably feels like a failure and like he doesn't fit in anywhere,"

"You know," Holly said, slowly nodding, "when we went to that LGBT+ party the other week. I was hardly getting sporty vibes from the place,"

Elliot completely agreed. Luca probably didn't feel like he fitted in anywhere. Not at home or with his family and certainly not with the stereotypical gay community here at the university. Hell, Elliot barely felt like he fitted in sometimes.

"I couldn't imagine what that feels like," Holly said.

"It isn't nice," Elliot said. "You feel like you… are just useless, not wanted and like the world is better off without you,"

Holy gasped. "Sorry. I forget you went through a rough patch,"

Elliot smiled, calling it a *rough patch* was an understatement but Elliot loved Holly too much to care.

"He mentioned something about charity work and wanting to prove to the world he's more than his sexuality," Elliot said.

"Makes sense. Isn't everyone more than their sexuality?"

Elliot was about to nod when a hot blond boy came over with Holly's chai latte and she seductively smiled at him and the hot boy blushed, but even that boy's smile wasn't as perfect as Luca's.

Damn it. Elliot was seriously into Luca and all he wanted to do was help make Luca feel wanted, respected and maybe even cared about, because Elliot was starting to realise he really did care about Luca.

"But I thought," Holly said, "he said that because he came from a homophobic family. Does he actually want the interview to be about proving he's more than his sexuality or pleasing his parents that don't want anyone to know he's gay?"

Elliot rolled his eyes.

He hated that wonderful Holly always made good points. It was probably why she always did the best in her essays, exams and other coursework assignments. She was a master at arguing and Elliot just knew she was going to make a hell of a journalist in the future.

But Elliot didn't really want to think about that right now. Not when the interview that could really help him after university was clearly going to fail.

Holly took out her phone and dialled a number.

"What you doing?" Elliot asked.

"Calling my friend Stacy. She runs the volunteering society. If Luca does charity work with the university she'll know," Holly said.

That would be amazing information to have.

"Hi Stacy," Holly said. "I'm good thanks. Do you know a Luca Pack? Does he do volunteering with you?"

Elliot just watched Holly and moved to the edge

of his seat to make sure he didn't miss a single detail. Not that he could hear what Stacy was saying on the phone.

"Okay. Brilliant. Thank you. And yes, I will come to your party on Friday. Bye," Holly said.

Elliot leant closer to her.

"Luca volunteers every single Saturday with that children home at the bottom of the hill for foster children, and every Sunday he volunteers at the Counselling Chambers in the city centre,"

Elliot's eyes widened. That was some serious charity work, because Elliot had had a foster brother and sister for a time, and they were amazing people. But Elliot also knew how much stigma and hate and negativity they received because they were fostered.

Elliot had wanted to foster some kids in the future to give them the respect, care and love that some foster children sadly didn't get, but the fact that Luca was actively helping them now was even more amazing.

And that really made Luca even more attractive.

"What's the Counselling Chambers?" Elliot asked. "It sounds familiar but I can't place it,"

Holly waved a finger as she was taking a hardy mouthful of her chai latte then she placed the mug down.

"It's a small charity in the city centre that offers free counselling to people who can't afford it and don't meet the requirements for the NHS. It mainly focuses on LGBT+, young and homeless people,"

Elliot just smiled. That actually was great news because it showed that Luca really wanted to connect with other gay people and help them, and it also showed that Luca was a good enough person to want to avoid going home when he could be doing charity work instead.

"I know that look," Holly said smiling. "You have your story,"

Elliot looked at her and slowly nodded. He actually did have his story and he really hoped that it would honour Luca, teach his homophobic parents a lesson and help Luca to know just how amazing he actually was.

But time was of the essence.

***

When Luca got back to his cold, lonely flat that was rather great normally but Luca really did feel sad, energised or even like he could enjoy anything at the moment as he threw himself onto his soft single bed that was cold as always with its thin blue bedsheets.

As Luca laid on his bed, partly enjoying the sweet scents of vanilla that came from them, he couldn't believe what he had just done, and how pathetic and stupid and silly he had been. There was absolutely no reason why he felt angry for those few precious seconds with beautiful Elliot.

All Elliot had tried to do was help himself, tell Luca the truth about him being perfect the way he was and Elliot was only slightly disapproving of how his parents and family had made him feel over the years.

Elliot was of course right about all of it, and that's exactly what had annoyed Luca so much. He wasn't used to people giving a damn about him, feeling anything for him and actually wanting to see if *he* was okay.

Normally everyone was only interested in their star football captain, the firstly openly gay boy to hold such a position and whatever nonsense Luca had to endure so the university and football society could tick their bloody diversity boxes.

All Luca actually wanted was for someone to tell him he was okay in the head, he was fine to be gay and at a real push, Luca would have loved someone to tell him he was beautiful. Luca didn't want anyone to tell him though, he was used to all the girls at the university telling him how hot he was, but Luca didn't want to be hot or seen as some hot model to fantasise over.

He wanted someone to find him beautiful for who he was, not his body.

Luca just realised that he had blown it with Elliot. He barely had any information to write his interview or article with. Luca had failed that cute, sweet boy that was only trying to help Luca and help his own future career, and Luca couldn't even be bothered to help him do that.

He was such a rubbish person.

Luca's laptop pinged.

Luca rolled his eyes because he always kept his

laptop open on his desk that was a few metres from his bed, and he really didn't want to answer any university emails at the moment.

It pinged again.

Luca seriously didn't need this but he forced himself to go over to his laptop and he was just a little confused that Elliot had emailed him with a link to an article.

Luca's stomach twisted into a painful knot. His shoulders and body tensed. This couldn't be happening.

He really hoped Elliot hadn't written an attacking, awful article about Luca's behaviour. That seriously wouldn't be good.

But Luca forced himself to take a few deep calming breaths and he clicked on the article link.

Luca was rather surprised when he saw the title of the article by Elliot. It was titled Why *Gays Are More Than Sexuality and Gay Footballers Are Amazing*.

Luca felt his entire body relax a little bit more as he read the article and he was amazed at how Elliot had found out some of the information. There was a lot of information about all the charity Luca did on the weekends and how it impacted so many lives, there was plenty of content about Luca's homophobic upbringing (even though this section never mentioned Luca's name specifically) and it really painted Luca in a very in-depth and positive light.

But Luca just focused on the very last paragraph. It was a sort of section praising and thanking Luca for agreeing to the interview, but also making Elliot more aware of problems that Luca had faced, but Luca just knew that the real point of the paragraph was to really hammer home exactly how great he was.

Luca had never had someone do this for him before. He had never had someone write things this nice about him, praising him for his charity, telling him that his parents and family were in the wrong and not him, and no one had ever called him amazing before.

Luca's stomach filled with butterflies and Luca realised that Elliot really was amazing.

Elliot could have written a harsher, "truer" article about how damaged, messed-up and useless Luca was and the real reason why he refused to give interviews, but he didn't. Elliot respected Luca and cared enough about him that he had gone the extra mile.

And all Luca could think about was if Elliot, the beautiful boy that he was, was willing to do that for Luca when they weren't even dating, talking or friends at the very least. What sort of amazing boyfriend could he be in the future?

That was a question Luca really wanted to answer.

And Luca seriously respected him for that, and then Luca checked the second email and it was Elliot asking if he liked it.

Luca wanted to write, scream and text, *yes* and tell beautiful Elliot exactly what this amazing article meant to him, but he almost didn't want to.

In fact Luca just realised that he really liked Elliot. He wasn't only a cute, beautiful boy but he was also kind, compassionate and really, really caring. Exactly the sort of guy that Luca wanted to be with, and ask out on a date.

Luca got up, grabbed his keys and went straight out of his apartment because that was exactly what he was going to do.

He had a very beautiful boy to ask out and that seriously excited him a lot more than he ever wanted to admit.

***

Elliot sat at a long row of fake-wooden desks along a long dull white wall in the university library with hundreds of rows of books behind him, giving the air a slight musty tang that made the taste of mustard form on his tongue, but Elliot didn't mind. He was far too happy at the moment.

He had sent off his article to his editor that had basically auto-published it, and he had sent a link to Luca.

The sheer silence of the library around him was a little off-putting because there were no other students in here with him, but Elliot just hoped that Luca liked it. When Elliot had sat down to write it, he had had no clue whatsoever what to write except from the charity work, but he just wrote and managed to pull it off.

All Elliot had really wanted to do was honour the pain, trauma and upset of Luca's past (and present as he presumably still lived with his parents during the university holidays), but Elliot also seriously wanted to tell Luca how amazing he was and that it was his parents that were in the wrong about his sexuality.

His editor liked the article, other students loved it judging by the comments and hell, Elliot had also received a few emails from national journalists (Elliot had a sneaking suspicion that his editor had emailed them about the article's publication), but Elliot still hadn't heard from the most important person.

The sweet scents of vanilla, hot chocolate and wonderful cinnamon filled the air and Elliot just knew that Holly was coming over because her strange perfume was what she always wore before a date, and it was weird that she was stopping off here before she went off.

Elliot turned around to see Holly walking away in her little black dress, but a very cute, sexy man was standing there waiting for him.

Luca looked flat out amazing, just in his white t-shirt from earlier that highlighted how fit, muscular and toned he was. He really was stunning, and all Elliot wanted to do in that moment was simply run his fingers through Luca's blond hair.

Elliot stared at Luca for a moment. Completely unsure of what he was going to say about the article. What if he was going to shout? Order him to delete it? What?

Luca rushed over to Elliot. Elliot tensed.

But Luca just hugged him and kissed him on the

cheek.

Elliot really loved the feeling of passion, care and attraction that flooded his body at the touch and Luca was seriously hugging him. and Elliot sort of got the feeling that this was the first time ever that Luca had truly hugged another man.

But it felt so right, natural and wonderful.

"Thank you," Luca said, still hugging Elliot tight. "I didn't mean to walk out on you earlier. I was angry at my life, my family and others. All-"

Elliot placed a finger over Luca's beautifully soft lips. "I know. All you wanted was for someone to tell you that you were right, wonderful and beautiful. I've been there, lots of people have been and you are really, really are beautiful,"

Elliot coughed a little as Luca hugged him even tighter and Elliot couldn't breathe.

"And you are amazing by the way," Elliot said, and gave Luca a little schoolboy smile. "I would love to hear about it more on a date,"

Luca pulled away a little, frowned and then smiled. "My first date? Yea, I would love that,"

Elliot gave Luca a quick amazing kiss on the cheek, their fingers interlinked and they slowly walked out of the library. And sure this was just a first date but Elliot knew it would go well because he really felt so connected to the beautiful man he was walking next to him.

And Elliot really hoped that this date would turn into another then another then hopefully that would lead to a lot more wonderful things down the road. And that was something Elliot was seriously looking forward to.

GAY UNIVERSITY ROMANCE COLLECTION VOLUME 2

GET YOUR FREE SHORT STORY NOW! And get signed up to Connor Whiteley's newsletter to hear about new gripping books, offers and exciting projects. (You'll never be sent spam)

https://www.subscribepage.com/gayromancesignup

About the author:

Connor Whiteley is the author of over 60 books in the sci-fi fantasy, nonfiction psychology and books for writer's genre and he is a Human Branding Speaker and Consultant.

He is a passionate warhammer 40,000 reader, psychology student and author.

Who narrates his own audiobooks and he hosts The Psychology World Podcast.

All whilst studying Psychology at the University of Kent, England.

Also, he was a former Explorer Scout where he gave a speech to the Maltese President in August 2018 and he attended Prince Charles' 70th Birthday Party at Buckingham Palace in May 2018.

Plus, he is a self-confessed coffee lover!

OTHER SHORT STORIES BY CONNOR WHITELEY

<u>Mystery Short Stories:</u>
Protecting The Woman She Hated
Finding A Royal Friend
Our Woman In Paris
Corrupt Driving
A Prime Assassination
Jubilee Thief
Jubilee, Terror, Celebrations
Negative Jubilation
Ghostly Jubilation
Killing For Womenkind
A Snowy Death
Miracle Of Death
A Spy In Rome
The 12:30 To St Pancreas
A Country In Trouble
A Smokey Way To Go
A Spicy Way To GO
A Marketing Way To Go
A Missing Way To Go
A Showering Way To Go
Poison In The Candy Cane
Christmas Innocence
You Better Watch Out
Christmas Theft
Trouble In Christmas
Smell of The Lake
Problem In A Car

Theft, Past and Team
Embezzler In The Room
A Strange Way To Go
A Horrible Way To Go
Ann Awful Way To Go
An Old Way To Go
A Fishy Way To Go
A Pointy Way To Go
A High Way To Go
A Fiery Way To Go
A Glassy Way To Go
A Chocolatey Way To Go
Kendra Detective Mystery Collection Volume 1
Kendra Detective Mystery Collection Volume 2
Stealing A Chance At Freedom
Glassblowing and Death
Theft of Independence
Cookie Thief
Marble Thief
Book Thief
Art Thief
Mated At The Morgue
The Big Five Whoopee Moments
Stealing An Election
Mystery Short Story Collection Volume 1
Mystery Short Story Collection Volume 2
Criminal Performance
Candy Detectives
Key To Birth In The Past

GAY UNIVERSITY ROMANCE COLLECTION VOLUME 2

<u>Science Fiction Short Stories:</u>
Temptation
Superhuman Autospy
Blood In The Redwater
All Is Dust
Vigil
Emperor Forgive Us
Their Brave New World
Gummy Bear Detective
The Candy Detective
What Candies Fear
The Blurred Image
Shattered Legions
The First Rememberer
Life of A Rememberer
System of Wonder
Lifesaver
Remarkable Way She Died
The Interrogation of Annabella Stormic
Blade of The Emperor
Arbiter's Truth
Computation of Battle
Old One's Wrath
Puppets and Masters
Ship of Plague
Interrogation
Edge of Failure
One Way Choice
Acceptable Losses
Balance of Power

Good Idea At The Time
Escape Plan
Escape In The Hesitation
Inspiration In Need
Singing Warriors
Knowledge is Power
Killer of Polluters
Climate of Death
The Family Mailing Affair
Defining Criminality
The Martian Affair
A Cheating Affair
The Little Café Affair
Mountain of Death
Prisoner's Fight
Claws of Death
Bitter Air
Honey Hunt
Blade On A Train

<u>Fantasy Short Stories:</u>
City of Snow
City of Light
City of Vengeance
Dragons, Goats and Kingdom
Smog The Pathetic Dragon
Don't Go In The Shed
The Tomato Saver
The Remarkable Way She Died
The Bloodied Rose
Asmodia's Wrath

GAY UNIVERSITY ROMANCE COLLECTION VOLUME 2

Heart of A Killer
Emissary of Blood
Dragon Coins
Dragon Tea
Dragon Rider
Sacrifice of the Soul
Heart of The Flesheater
Heart of The Regent
Heart of The Standing
Feline of The Lost
Heart of The Story
City of Fire
Awaiting Death

Other books by Connor Whiteley:
Bettie English Private Eye Series
A Very Private Woman
The Russian Case
A Very Urgent Matter
A Case Most Personal
Trains, Scots and Private Eyes
The Federation Protects

Lord of War Origin Trilogy:
Not Scared Of The Dark
Madness
Burn It All

The Fireheart Fantasy Series
Heart of Fire
Heart of Lies
Heart of Prophecy
Heart of Bones
Heart of Fate

City of Assassins (Urban Fantasy)
City of Death
City of Marytrs
City of Pleasure
City of Power

Agents of The Emperor
Return of The Ancient Ones
Vigilance
Angels of Fire
Kingmaker
The Eight
The Lost Generation

Lord Of War Trilogy (Agents of The Emperor)
Not Scared Of The Dark
Madness
Burn It All Down

The Garro Series- Fantasy/Sci-fi
GARRO: GALAXY'S END
GARRO: RISE OF THE ORDER
GARRO: END TIMES
GARRO: SHORT STORIES

GAY UNIVERSITY ROMANCE COLLECTION VOLUME 2

GARRO: COLLECTION
GARRO: HERESY
GARRO: FAITHLESS
GARRO: DESTROYER OF WORLDS
GARRO: COLLECTIONS BOOK 4-6
GARRO: MISTRESS OF BLOOD
GARRO: BEACON OF HOPE
GARRO: END OF DAYS

Winter Series- Fantasy Trilogy Books
WINTER'S COMING
WINTER'S HUNT
WINTER'S REVENGE
WINTER'S DISSENSION

Miscellaneous:
RETURN
FREEDOM
SALVATION
Reflection of Mount Flame
The Masked One
The Great Deer

Gay Romance Novellas
Breaking, Nursing, Repairing A Broken Heart
Jacob And Daniel
Fallen For A Lie
His Heartstopper
Spying And Weddings

www.ingramcontent.com/pod-product-compliance
Lightning Source LLC
LaVergne TN
LVHW012112070526
838202LV00056B/5697